"I will not be persuaded against my better judgment! Why will you persist so, my lord? You must allow me to say no!"

"You say it frequently, Miss Fielding."

She had forgotten how those swift rejoinders could take the wind out of her sails. He was still the Viscount Spendale who had abducted her and teased her, still incalculable. He surprised her yet again, for he was looking down at her with an expression which made her heart beat faster.

"I cannot let you go, Eliane. I must—must believe that you will come to care for me—"

Also by Katharine Flixton:

LYTTON ABBEY

GLENGARRICK'S HEIR

Katharine Flixton

FAWCETT CREST • NEW YORK

A Fawcett Crest Book
Published by Ballantine Books
Copyright © 1970 by Katharine Flixton

All rights reserved under International and Pan-American Copyright Conventions. Published in the United States by Ballantine Books, a division of Random House, Inc., New York, and simultaneously in Canada by Random House of Canada Limited, Toronto. Originally published in Great Britain by Robert Hale Ltd. in 1970.

ISBN 0-449-21884-8

Manufactured in the United States of America

First Ballantine Books Edition: August 1990

CHAPTER ONE

The joyous, shouting mob of people surged forward to gain admittance to Vauxhall Gardens. As their hackney coachman endeavored to force a way through, Miss Eliane Fielding grew more cheerful. It was impossible not to respond to the mood of the pleasure-seeking crowd, and she began to feel that the evening might after all not prove too bad, even though she must hope that Mrs. Benson's vulgarities would be sufficient that night to cure even Ned of his unfortunate infatuation. It already looked as though this might be so, and that her half brother would be disillusioned even before their parents became aware of his entanglement, for Amelia was undoubtedly in fine form.

Nevertheless, it looked also as though the evening might provide problems. Until they started out, Miss Fielding had not realized that Mr. Dick Hewitt, being Mrs. Benson's brother, might prove on further acquaintance to be as odious as his sister and a hazard to herself. She had already had to flutter her fan continuously to protect herself from his too ardent gaze, and she could not even be sure that the proximity of his foot to her own was entirely accidental. She could only hope that once inside the gardens, the general entertainment would be sufficient to distract him.

Now, as they descended from the hackney and began to thread their way through the chattering throng, the vivacious Amelia became inspired at the prospect of rubbing shoulders with the world of rank and fashion, which she loudly assured them one could do better at Vauxhall than anywhere else in the world!

Her voice became louder and more affected as she looked around to see what acquaintances she might claim amongst the fashionables in the crowd. Miss Fielding suspected that she knew none, and felt relieved. Amelia, however, had caught sight of a small group of elegantly dressed persons and pushed her way toward them. She dared not claim acquaintance with them, but she made sure that they and every one else within earshot heard her vow and declare that as she lived, they should see many friends there that night!

"I vow, Mr. Page, we could not have chosen a better night! The Pantheon would have been but dull compared with this! Miss Fielding, are not those lanterns the prettiest you ever saw? Dick, you shall obtain the finest box that you may!"

Thus Amelia. Some of the humbler persons looked impressed. One or two better-dressed people had glanced at her flamboyant dress of cerise and violet trimmed with emerald green ribbons and her badly powdered elaborate coiffure, and had quickly lost interest or laughed. Miss Fielding closed her eyes.

When she opened them again, she saw that Amelia was endeavoring to attract the attention of a tall young exquisite, to be rewarded by a brief stare of the utmost indifference. The young man's glance then fell upon the other lady of Mrs. Benson's party, and Miss Fielding, although looking very different from Amelia, fared little better with him. His look merely changed to a bold, significant admiration, until the color rose in her cheeks, and she turned away foolishly to speak with false animation to Mr. Hewitt.

Amelia's brother plainly regarded her sudden interest as encouragement, and she paid for this during the whole of supper. The box he procured for them was not where rank and fashion foregathered. The Vauxhall servants had been quick to sum up Mr. Hewitt as a person of no importance, and they had been allotted a box in an obscure corner. Miss Fielding would not have minded this, having no wish to encounter another such gaze from any other fashionable young buck.

As she sat now in the gaily painted box at some distance from the orchestra, Eliane grew less and less confident that her desire for a commonsense solution to Ned's entanglement had led her to the wisest course. She wished heartily that Mrs. Benson and her opulent charms had never entered her stepmother's shop in Soho with such disastrous effects upon Ned. She fluttered her fan vigorously to avoid Mr. Hewitt, and glanced across the crowd of promenaders. The fan stopped abruptly in the most betraying fashion, and then hastily resumed. The young man dressed in the height of fashion whom she had seen earlier was now leaning back negligently against a lantern-lit tree, keeping their box under amused observation.

Was ever there such insolence? thought Eliane. Yet were they not asking for such attention?

As the famous soprano began to sing and the promenaders stopped respectfully to listen, Miss Fielding forced her charming face to betray nothing but a rapt interest in the song.

A swift glance beneath her long lashes showed that he was still there, having apparently left his own party, seeming to listen to the song also, but making her so very aware of him. She feared he knew that, too. As he lounged there against the tree, his whole bearing one of easy self-assurance, she had little doubt that he was deliberately teasing her.

The song was followed by an encore, but at last that part of the concert and the applause that followed it were ended. People began to move again, and once more Amelia's clarion affectations sounded across the Gardens.

"Miss Fielding, pray let us take a stroll in the groves where we may hear the nightingales. Then we may return for the fireworks!"

Eliane did not demur, but rose willingly to her feet....

In one of the very best boxes which Vauxhall could provide, another very pretty young lady was also endeavoring to hide her vexation. Unlike Mrs. Benson, Miss Juliet Lawley although so newly come to London did know many of the people of rank and fashion who were present, and she did not care for the fact that they could see that Spendale had absented himself from their party for the best part of an hour. Really, he had no manners!

This of course, although a satisfying condemnation which soothed her feelings, was not wholly true. Spendale's manners when he chose were as impeccable as his breeding. He could also be equally rude when it suited him.

"Ah, Miss Lawley! Your servant, Ma'am. I had thought Lord Spendale to be one of your party. Did I not see him earlier?"

Thus the Hon. Herbert Norrey. The old gossip, thought Juliet. Putting it down in his diary, no doubt. He never missed a thing, and she did not doubt that all the world knew her desire to secure Lord Spendale's interest. Indeed, she had not bothered to conceal it, since she had always got what she wanted, and she had not expected such a signal lack of success as she was now encountering.

When she had first come to England from her father's estates in Virginia, a pretty redhead with provincial ways and great social ambitions, she had made the acquaintance in Bristol of Lord Spendale's brother, the Honorable Neil Ardmore. She had even imagined herself a little in love with him, for he was a tall and strikingly handsome young man, with a pleasant disposition which won him many friends. Her rapid conquest of Neil Ardmore had led her to expect the same success with his brother. However, as dark and unpredictable as Neil was fair and even-tempered, Lord Spendale had proved annoyingly resistant to her charms. Her fortune could not tempt him, for the Ardmore family were wealthy, and it was well known that Spendale had his own resources, but she had seen no reason to play the demure miss in order to captivate him, and her attempts to provoke him out of his indifference were already causing some amusement and speculation.

She answered the Hon. Herbert Norrey as brightly as she could. Fortunately their party was large enough for his lordship's defection not to embarrass her too much. Lady Herrick, who was one of Mr. Norrey's party, laughed a little. "Lord Spendale is a law unto himself. If you expect him to oblige anyone except Spendale then you must think again. Be warned, Miss Lawley!"

Juliet forced a smile. Lady Herrick would have an interest in warning her thus, since she was hoping that Miss Lawley would favor her son, who was one of the many who were dancing attendance upon her and her American fortune. Juliet, however, had increasingly no eyes for anyone but that arrogant young man who seemed to go out of his way to rebuff her, but whose bride, when he chose her, would one day become Countess of Glengarrick. To Juliet it was a dazzling prospect.

At this precise moment, however, it was convenient to bestow an encouraging smile upon Mr. Roger Herrick while awaiting Lord Spendale's return....

Alastair Ardmore, Viscount Spendale, heir to the Earl of Glengarrick, had strolled through the groves preferring his own thoughts to the continued company of Juliet Lawley and the rest of their party. Juliet's determined pursuit of himself bored him. He had not been greatly attracted when she first came upon the town, the latest heiress and for once an undeniably pretty one. He did not care for red-haired women, and this one was—regrettably, he thought, the one his brother wanted. If he himself had any preference at all, it was for dazzling blondes. He had not contemplated giving a second thought to the noisy creature who had endeavored to catch his eye at the entrance to Vauxhall. Although now perversely bent upon one of his diversions from the world of fashion, he was fastidious enough not to be attracted to Mrs. Benson.

The other one, he thought, had been better. Nothing remarkable to his first glance, with his mind still upon the superior charms of blondes, but reasonable features and smoothly brushed dark curls. There had been a neatness about her which pleased him. A flawless skin which had colored up rosily when he looked at her. A milliner's apprentice or a seamstress, he thought, just learning her powers of attraction, and resenting the noisy self-assurance of the other woman.

His own party were quickly served with their supper, and he had chosen to leave them without a word. He cared little what they might make of that. He invariably pleased himself, caring little whether it enraged others. He knew that Mrs. Ross, Juliet Lawley's chaperone and guide through the London season, did not like him. He cared nothing for that, either, although he had some respect for Mrs. Ross. He was only interested in an evening's devilment such as his father would not have approved of, and as he sauntered past the boxes during the concert, he caught sight of the quartet whose behavior had attracted his attention earlier.

They amused him now as he stayed to lean against the lantern-lit tree and observe them. The little brunette, who was little only as she might appear against his own height, was plainly not enjoying the attentions of the other man, a flashy creature more suited, surely, to the blonde. The boy, however, seemed besotted on the older woman. He hung admiringly upon every word she uttered so noisily, while the dark girl grew obviously more and more dissatisfied with her evening's entertainment and the defection of her young lover. Moreover she was now, he knew, aware of himself, however much she tried to conceal it behind the flutterings of her fan. The hunter in him was aroused. He thought he could offer her better entertainment.

As they arose, and departed from their box, Spendale straightened himself with lazy grace and moved after them. He had now decided upon his quarry for the evening, and she would make a pleasant change from Juliet, who would, he thought shrewdly, now salve her vanity by encouraging Roger Herrick.

In the groves, Mrs. Benson was plainly inviting Ned to seek her company alone, and the pair of them quickly set off into another grove, leaving Mr. Hewitt and Miss Fielding alone. Most of the other people in the Gardens had already gone to watch the firework display which was soon to commence, and the paths were comparatively deserted. Miss Fielding had not realized this, and had mistakenly supposed herself safer from the attentions of Mr. Hewitt as they walked than she had been in the close confines of the supper box. She soon realized her mistake, however, as she had to fend him off from snatching a kiss. This was a thing she had not bestowed upon any man yet, and she had no intention of allowing Mr. Hewitt to be the first.

Suddenly Mr. Hewitt's grip slackened, and he went down upon the graveled path in all his cheap finery in a way which delighted Miss Fielding. She glanced up gratefully at her rescuer, and then saw with some misgiving who it was.

"I—I thank you, sir." Her color deepened as her humiliation increased.

Lord Spendale liked her voice, a thing he had not, from experience, expected. He bowed very gallantly, and offered her his arm, but she did not take it.

"Perhaps you would prefer to return to your box," he said. "Or to take a walk, without this gentleman?"

Eliane looked unwillingly at "this gentleman," but Mr. Hewitt, on picking himself up, thought better of offering retaliation. He very rightly judged from the look and sound of the newcomer that he wore a sword not as an unaccustomed decoration but as a weapon he knew well how to use. Mr. Hewitt therefore hurried away without a word, leaving the haughty Miss Fielding to her fate.

She was not sure of the young man's intentions. His manner had until now hardly been respectful. She was under no illusions how she must appear to him, seeing her in the company of the flamboyant Amelia and her horrid brother. Where was Ned? She must find him and insist upon their going home. She had had enough of this evening, and Mr. Hewitt must look after his sister.

"I must find my brother," she said.

So the besotted young fool was a brother, not a lover! There was no resemblance that he could see. Spendale walked beside her until they came to a seat in an arbor, speculating swiftly on his next move to detain her. At that moment, there was a tremendous hiss of igniting fireworks, and the whole sky was lit with brilliant cascades of color. Miss Fielding gasped, and looked up involuntarily. The showers of colored light were falling gracefully earthward, but Lord Spendale had seen many such shows before. He was looking with pleasure upon her upturned face, realizing that she was far prettier than he had at first thought, and that there was only one thing to do to parted lips of such perfection.

For the second time within minutes, Miss Fielding found herself in a man's arms. This time there was no escape. Spendale had not Mr. Hewitt's tentative approach. He held her with easy strength, and kissed her as he would have kissed any other girl he picked up in a public garden. He intended to stir his little beauty into a suitable response.

Eliane struggled violently. At last he released his hold, and smiled down at her. Instantly she broke free and dealt him a stinging slap across the face. He in turn was surprised at the strength she put into it. It was no token of respectable resistance. Miss Fielding was expressing all her outrage and fury at the events of the evening.

At that moment, Miss Lawley strolling with her companions and recognizing his lordship and hearing the slap at the same time, broke into a peal of laughter which she fully intended Spendale should hear. It was her way of repaying him for his desertion of herself and her party.

Spendale heard, and recognized the laugh. He looked down at Miss Fielding's pretty face, now tense with shock and anger, and was once again aware of her surprising voice, which was shaking, but which showed that she was accustomed to speaking with persons of quality.

"How *dared* you? I wish—I wish—"

"Yes, Ma'am?" His hazel eyes glinted challengingly. She was not to know that he was displeased that Miss Lawley had seen his rebuff, which at any other time would only have made him laugh.

"I wish I had a brother to call you out—or give you the drubbing you deserve!" Her voice was trembling, and she drew out from her dress a small laceedged handkerchief and scrubbed at her mouth with it. With an air of angry contempt, she flung it then upon the ground as if she would disdain to touch it again, and then turned and hurried away, seeing with relief that Ned and Mrs. Benson had reappeared, even if with the odious Mr. Hewitt.

Spendale thought for a moment to follow her, but he saw that she had regained her companions, who were showing concern for her distress.

A drubbing! He thought cynically of the word she used. High-ropes for a seamstress! She took herself very seriously, whoever she was. His mouth twitched in amusement. More likely this high-sounding phraseology was for his special benefit. His amusement was lessened only by the fact that Juliet Lawley had seen the encounter. He touched his cheek thoughtfully, bent down and retrieved the handkerchief, and smiling, thrust it into his coat pocket. He was well aware that Juliet was watching. Roger Herrick, too. Then he straightened himself, and with no apparent loss of composure, went to rejoin them.

"Miss Lawley," his glance flickered over Juliet, faintly mocking as always. He offered her his arm, ignoring Mr. Herrick. "Are you not going to watch the fireworks?"

She could not resist. "It seems there is better entertainment here within the groves," she said unwisely.

"True—" He chose to turn and watch for a moment the girl speaking to her friends at the far end of the path. He was still smiling a little, and Juliet was piqued.

"An apprentice, or a servant, I suppose?" she said contemptuously.

"A very pretty girl," he corrected. "The prettiest I have seen tonight."

Juliet colored angrily, but she was already wishing she had not tried to disconcert him. With Neil Ardmore she had been instantly at ease, never seeming to put a foot wrong, but how different it was with Spendale! She knew his reputation for being hard and unpredictable, and he could make her uneasy. She wished she had not laughed quite so loudly.

Miss Fielding now desired to hurry away from Vauxhall more than ever. Ned was all for offering to fight her assailant, but when she expressed her angry wish for a brother to call out that hateful young man, she had not been thinking of Ned, whose skill in spite of his proudly worn sword was likely to be negligible. She guessed, as had Mr. Hewitt, that her tormentor, coming from the class he did, was likely to be an accomplished swordsman who could run Ned through in a minute.

"No—no—make no more of it," she said agitatedly. "Let us return home, if you please!"

They made their way to the gates, and Ned hurried to obtain a hackney to take their party home. Mr. Hewitt was in a huff, and determined to let all be aware of it. Had she been capable of appreciating it at the moment, Miss Fielding might have been cheered to know that Ned had indeed begun to be disenchanted by Amelia. Already it seemed to him that his sister's distress and her desire to keep the whole matter from their parents' knowledge was in marked contrast to Amelia's desire to make the most of it. She wondered loudly and frequently who the offender was, sure that he must be a gentleman of rank, judging by his clothes and his self-assurance. She recalled in detail the party he had been with, and while to her oddly quiet companions she loudly condemned the licentiousness of such behavior, she left even Ned with the impression that she would have responded very differently had she been so assaulted herself.

As for Lord Spendale, a perverse pride made him return to his own party and face it out with Miss Lawley, who had so tactlessly witnessed his discomfiture and so foolishly advertised her amusement at it. Had he followed his own instinctive inclination, he would have discreetly kept Miss Fielding's party under observation and possibly followed to find out where she lived, because he was more intrigued than he had hoped for by the girl. But it was only a repressed instinct, not close enough to the surface to be stronger than the momentary need to stare Miss Lawley out of countenance.

During the days that followed, he found himself wishing he had pursued the Vauxhall girl and her friends. For him, an evening's amusement, no more remarkable than other occasions, had had an unexpected sequel. He could not get the girl out of his mind. She had not been like the others. Her delicate face, her unexpected voice, something about her would not let him alone. He began to look for her everywhere in London, although he thought he would not find her in his own world, not if her Vauxhall companions were anything to judge by.

CHAPTER TWO

ALTHOUGH Miss Fielding had referred to Ned Page as her brother, they were in fact not related at all. When Charles Fielding had been left a widower with an infant daughter, he had mourned his wife for some years, and would have preferred to remain faithful to her memory but for the fact that he was an unworldly scholar who needed someone to look after his child. Neither expecting nor wishing to feel the same passion for another woman that he had for Eliane's mother, he had been glad to take advantage of the encouragement given him by Mrs. Mary Page, a widow with a son even younger than his own daughter, and a substantial haberdasher's business in the city.

On setting up house for her second marriage, the new Mrs. Fielding had removed her business to Soho, and taken a handsome double-fronted shop with living premises above and a good garden behind, in one of the streets off Soho Square. It was a proceeding which proved to be perfectly harmonious for all concerned. Mr. Fielding, although quiet and of little use in business affairs, was a man of good sense and authority, and his second wife was pleased to defer to him in all but the running of the shop, in which he took no interest. As for Eliane, whose mother had been French, and who had been brought up to a fluency in that tongue, she had grown up into a quiet, reserved girl who never gave her stepmother cause for concern.

Ned was a different matter. He was prone to enthusiasms. For a while he had desired to be a soldier, while his stepfather had wished him to go to Oxford. Meanwhile, he helped his mother run their haberdashery business, and did not altogether seem to dislike it. His sister thought privately that Ned never would be the scholar her father hoped, and would eventually settle down in business.

The morning after the Vauxhall visit, Eliane came down late to breakfast. She was rarely in the shop herself. Mrs. Fielding and Ned rose early and saw to the opening of the shop before they joined Mr. Fielding and his daughter for breakfast.

Mrs. Fielding looked shrewdly at her stepdaughter's pale face and remarked that the two of them had returned earlier from Vauxhall than she had expected. Did they not stay until the end?

Ned opened his mouth, glanced at his sister, and then shut it again as he received a sharp kick on the ankle.

"I had a headache, Mamma," said Eliane, "and found it rather noisy in the crowds. We decided to leave early."

"I hope your friends were not too disappointed," said Mr. Fielding courteously. He had not met Mrs. Benson and her brother, and as Eliane knew, would not have approved of them if he had. She hoped that she and Ned had seen the last of that pair.

"Never mind," said Ned cheerfully. "I'll take you and Maria to the Pantheon next week. There is a masked ball to be held there. I can go tomorrow for tickets."

Eliane felt some relief. Ned was obviously about to veer once more toward Maria Taylor, the object of his affections when he was not interested in someone like Amelia Benson. Eliane and Maria were not wholly intimate, since Eliane was as reserved as Maria was open and brash, but the two girls liked each other. Maria's parents kept a milliner's establishment nearby which was much patronized by the fashionable world, and it suddenly occurred to Eliane that Maria from her knowledge of her father's customers was much more likely to know the identity of her assailant in Vauxhall than would Amelia Benson. However, she had no intention of telling Maria what had happened, and she did not really think that she would ever see him again, for which she told herself she was profoundly thankful.

It seemed that the tranquillity of the Fielding household was no longer in danger, and as for the Vauxhall episode, she thought it would be a very long time before she went there again. Having dismissed that insolent young man from her mind, and no longer expecting to see him around every corner, she resumed her expeditions with her father and with Maria, who frequently accompanied her to church and to walks in the park.

On these occasions it was impossible not to enjoy Maria's company. Eliane had done her best to share her father's scholarly pursuits, but she was also a very normal girl interested in clothes and fashion, and where better to see fashion than as it was displayed by the wealth and rank of London? Maria knew so much about what they saw. From the maids who accompanied their ladies to the Taylors' shop, she procured back copies of the *Ladies' Magazine* and other periodicals, including the *Gazette* and the *Advertiser*, and she knew, or as Eliane sometimes suspected, invented, a great deal about the lives of fashionable people.

One morning some weeks later, Maria called at the Fielding home to say that her mother wished her to deliver a hatbox to a house in Grosvenor Square, and she would be glad of Eliane's company, for they might then go on to watch the riders in Hyde Park.

The hatbox delivered, the two girls went on to the park, admiring the beautiful horses and the ladies and gentlemen who rode them with such grace and skill. On these occasions Maria was never averse to catching the eye of any respectable stroller, although she knew that Miss Fielding never behaved so, and nothing ever came of it.

This morning, having seen something that caught her interest, Maria turned to speak to Eliane, and was surprised to see her self-possessed friend blushing vividly, and looked to see the cause.

A fashionably dressed young man had moved away from the group of riders with whom he had been speaking, and now bowed deeply to them.

"Eliane!" Maria was a creature of impulse and few inhibitions. Her astonishment at this actual happening of the sort of thing she had dreamed about made her voice rise audibly. Too audibly for Miss Fielding's comfort. Maria's young voice had never had its carrying power so marked. "It is Lord Spendale! And he is bowing to *us*!"

Miss Fielding's embarrassment grew. He must have heard! Was she always to be put out of countenance? Maria was only being Maria, but what an unfortunate encounter! She declined to bow in acknowledgment, but quickened her step, only to find him in her path.

So he was a lord! With all the bold and selfish arrogance Eliane had come to expect, at least in theory, from the aristocracy, be they French or English.

"Miss Fielding, I believe? Your most obedient and humble servant, Ma'am."

How dared he humiliate her by so obviously recognizing her? And how did he know her name? It was her first experience of the fact that he seldom forgot anything. Mrs. Benson had called her Miss Fielding at the entrance to Vauxhall Gardens and he had remembered it.

Eliane would not even look at him, after that first breathless moment of recognition. He was every whit as tall, as handsome, as completely at his ease, as she remembered him. She wished herself miles away. No more would she accompany Maria Taylor on these expeditions if this were to happen!

He saw from her face that she would not, for the moment, speak to him, and that he would fare better with the girl at her side.

"Will you not at least introduce me to your friend, Miss Fielding?" he said imperturbably. "I think I had not the pleasure of meeting her also at Vauxhall?"

At the sheer effrontery of that "also," Eliane breathed deeply and remained mute. Maria, however, was delighted, and nothing loth obliged his lordship with her name, and gave him what she hoped was the most elegant of curtsies. She was rewarded by the most elegant of bows. Maria was astonished that Eliane should be so chilling and distant, and wondered how she had become thus acquainted with a member of the nobility?

His lordship found that his pretty victim was not to be intimidated into accepting him.

"I do not know this gentleman. There is a mistake." And she walked on, expecting Maria to follow. Lord Spendale smiled winningly upon Miss Taylor. "One day, Miss Taylor, I hope that Miss Fielding will speak to me. But are you unattended? Perhaps I may accompany you? Have you far to go?"

Such attention from the ranks of her father's customers made Maria a little dizzy, but she was also nervous. She dared not let the resolutely disappearing Miss Fielding from her sight. Stammering, she thanked him and said that she must hurry after Miss Fielding. They had not far to go. Only to Soho Square.

He thought it a fair distance for them, but knew better than to persist. He bowed, having what he wanted, an idea where she lived. He thought he could proceed from there. He professed himself Miss Taylor's servant and said he hoped to see her in the park again.

Maria bobbed another curtsy and hurried after Miss Fielding.

"Eliane! Oh, stop! I declare I am out of breath. Must you go so fast? My dear, he would have walked with us had I allowed him! How people would envy us! How came you to be acquainted with him? It is plain he thinks he has offended you, but he is politeness itself, Eliane!"

"Oh, indeed," said Miss Fielding ironically, but she continued to walk swiftly lest he follow them. But he did not. Maria could not forbear to turn back a second, to see that he had returned to the group of riders.

From the park to Soho Maria talked incessantly. Eliane did not seem sufficiently impressed by her good fortune. He was so handsome, had such an air, any girl Maria knew would be crazed to get a look from him....

"Well, I am not," said Miss Fielding with unwonted shortness.

"He is plainly attracted to you," protested Maria. "Can you not be a little excited?"

"No, I cannot. And what do you imagine such a gentleman could have to do with anyone in our station of life? There is no possible good that can come of such an acquaintance as you are envisaging, Maria, so pray be sensible. And we will say nothing of this to anyone, if you please."

She meant sincerely what she said, and Maria having at last reluctantly agreed, Eliane could not resist a question before the subject was, she hoped, finally abandoned.

"Who did you say he was, Maria? It is not a name I have heard."

"To be sure, you are so seldom in your own shop," said Maria, who sometimes thought that Mrs. Fielding made too much of a lady of Eliane. "I have seen him before, and who would forget him? He is the Viscount Spendale, and is heir to the Earl of Glengarrick. I think that is in Scotland." She sighed. "They say he has an eye for the ladies, and indeed, I have heard some of our customers gossiping of him. He is certainly interested in you, Eliane. How did he come to know your name?"

Eliane could well believe that he had such a reputation. She did not answer Maria's question directly, but only repeated her former statement with some severity, as she detected a note of wistfulness in Maria's voice. "People of his rank can have nothing to do with you and me—not—not that way! You would be very foolish to think otherwise."

Once more Maria agreed, but to be bowed to—to be admired by a member of the highest society! She wished her friend were not always so remote. Maria believed herself to be very fond of Ned's half sister, but there was no doubt she could be chill and daunting, not always seeing eye to eye with Maria over what was allowable. Maria had always supposed it to be due to Mr. Fielding being such a scholarly gentleman and to Eliane's own mother being French. That was another odd thing about Eliane. She could not ever be prevailed upon to speak of her French mother.

Maria sighed again at the thought of his lordship. She had no real wish to be sensible and to stop and think what good or ill might come from an acquaintance with an admiring young aristocrat. She was already imagining herself meeting him at a masked ball or at Ranelagh, if she could prevail upon Ned to take her there. However, she good-naturedly promised Eliane that she would say nothing of this surprising encounter to anyone at home, and Eliane knew she could trust her. Maria was a good and loyal girl at heart, and would make a good wife for Ned, she thought.

When he was the sole member of his family in London, Lord Spendale preferred to keep in lodgings, but now that his brother was prolonging his stay in order to be near Juliet Lawley, and their sister Ailsa was expected from Scotland with Aunt Kirsty to keep an eye on her, permission had been obtained from their father to open the Ardmore town house near the Green Park.

He now walked from St. James in a better mood than had been usual for some time. He had found the girl again, and he liked her metal. If she were merely pretending to be distant, he would soon lose interest in her. That tactic never deceived him long. As for her general manner, he could not place her. Miss Maria Taylor was easy enough to place, although different again from that appalling creature the girl had been with at Vauxhall. Why was she so different from those she consorted with? She spoke like a lady. Could she be an actress? He would swear he had never seen her on the London stage, but if she were, her pursuit and capture should offer little difficulty. And what had the Taylor wench called her? Mary-Ann? Sally-Ann?

She had smacked his face. Well, it was not the first time that had happened to him, although in this instance he would have preferred that the tiresome Miss Lawley had not witnessed it. He did not pay Mr. Roger Herrick the compliment of a second thought, but Juliet, he thought, would have to be dealt with soon.

Spendale thought it a pity that his brother should be so taken with the heiress's attractions. Neil as a second son would have to make his own way in the world, and to look for money was natural enough, but Neil was not likely to put money first. It seemed as if his affections were truly engaged, and since he had a notable obstinacy of purpose, his affections once given were not likely to be switched elsewhere. Unless, mused Alastair Ardmore, Neil came to be sickened finally by her brazen pursuit of himself. It was a pity that Miss Juliet Lawley could not see that Neil had a great many virtues that Lord Spendale had not... except perhaps, he thought cynically, the prospect of an earldom.

He walked up the steps of Ardmore House, and was admitted by the waiting footman. He found Neil in the morning room, still in his riding clothes, and Spendale, looking at him, once again thought Juliet a misguided fool. The Hon. Neil Ardmore, two years younger than his brother, but not looking it, was all of six-feet two, with all the Ardmore good looks of regular features and fair hair and blue eyes. Neil and Meg, now married, took after their father. He himself, the eldest and Ailsa the youngest, took after their mother.

Thinking momentarily of Ailsa, so soon to descend upon them, he wondered from whence they got their temperament. There was a saying "to quarrel vilely like an Ardmore," but there had been plenty of cussedness on both sides of the family, if what he had heard of his parents' early courtship was true.

"Well, Neil, did you buy that horse?"

"No, I had second thoughts. I prefer the one that Slaney's offering, even if it means going up to Newmarket again. I'm after it tomorrow."

"Did you see Juliet?"

"We went riding in Richmond Park." Neil was otherwise uncommunicative. "When is Ailsa due? Have you heard?"

"This week, I imagine. With Aunt Kirsty. A most unsuitable arrangement. Ailsa has always been able to twist our good aunt around her little finger. I am surprised at mother. She must be relying upon us! Aunt Kirsty might have managed Ailsa in Edinburgh, but not in London!"

"It would no doubt have been better to have left her with Meg in Leicestershire," said Neil reflectively. "But Meg will be in no condition to deal with Ailsa's tricks. So it falls upon you, brother," he added with good-natured mockery.

"Thank you for nothing."

Lord Spendale wondered a little how much looking after his young sister would curtail his own activities. He was looking forward to the pursuit and possession of the pretty Miss Fielding, and would have preferred not to have had the Lady Ailsa in Town for a week or so. However, his good humor continued. When she arrived with Lady Bray a week later, he greeted his sister with real affection. They had stopped a few days in Leicestershire to see Lady Margaret and Mr. Thomas Denby, but Ailsa was all agog to reach town, and found Leicestershire dull with Meg not unnaturally preoccupied with the imminent arrival of her firstborn.

Spendale continued his round of pleasures. He was, like Miss Lawley, accustomed to getting what he wanted, and he had no reason to suppose that he would fail with his pretty charmer from Vauxhall. That she was not in the common run was obvious, but from his experience there was no reason to think that the acquaintance would not ripen to the outcome he was beginning to envisage. So far he had been a casual amorist. Marriage was a serious matter for the future Earl of Glengarrick. Spendale had all his family's pride of race, and did not expect to marry out of his own rank. No doubt some suitable and well-dowered young woman would stir him sufficiently for him to offer, but for the moment he had no thought of marriage.

The Vauxhall girl had shown him that she was

not the amusement for one night he had at first imagined from her being with such vulgar companions. He had begun to think of the pleasures of spending longer in her company, perhaps in the Hampstead villa he had inherited from his mother's uncle, Sir Ronald Gordon. It was a substantial house, elegantly furnished, and soon to be let to a suitable tenant with whom the Glengarrick steward was even now negotiating. The prospective let could easily be canceled and Miss Fielding installed in the villa if she should prove willing, and he thought that in spite of her resistance so far, she would soften.

He realized that he had behaved a little too brashly at Vauxhall and offended her. He would see how suitable apologies would advance his cause.

There now began for Miss Eliane Fielding a very trying time. Lord Spendale seemed to be frequently in the neighborhood of Dane Street. This was of course an illusion, since he was a very busy idler, and had many social commitments, especially now that his younger sister had arrived in Town, but it had been a disagreeable shock to find him in the Taylors' millinery establishment, helping to choose hats for the two fashionably dressed young ladies who were with him. She had gone to speak to Maria, and had hastily withdrawn when she saw who was in the shop, but not before he had seen her, and had seen her confusion at the sight of himself. No doubt because of the young ladies he had made no move to come and speak to her, but she had felt the blatant interest of his regard.

Then Maria Taylor had received an anonymous gift of tickets for a masked ball at the Opera House, and since Maria could not imagine, so she said, who had sent them, Miss Fielding felt that she might guess a little. Naturally she declined to go, but Maria went with Ned, and came back to say that Lord Spendale had been there, and expressed disappointment at not seeing Miss Fielding.

Next she found herself confronted by him as she came from church in Soho Square. Since it was so near her home, she did not always take Molly the maid with her, but now wished she did not appear alone. He gave her a low bow, professed himself her most humble and obedient, most admiring servant, but compelled her to halt amongst the dispersing worshipers.

"Will you not relent and speak to me?" he said with a smile.

"I have no wish to speak with you!"

"Do you know that you have the loveliest voice," he said. "I wish I might hear it say kinder things."

She breathed deeply, and the lovely voice shook a little.

"Will you cease to pester me? It is intolerable!"

Amusement flickered in the handsome face. "A hard word to use to one who admires you to distraction, Miss Fielding. Dare I say one who adores you, even though you rebuff me?"

Her dark blue eyes flashed with temper at his persistence. "Pray occupy yourself in some way that does not concern me!" she snapped.

"So unrelenting?"

She did not answer, and bending a little closer, he said softly: "You catch me more than you know, Miss Fielding."

"I find *you* detestable!" she said swiftly.

He stood aside then, to let her go, and she could only hope that now he would lose interest in her.

The next week gave her cause to hope that this

was so, since it passed without her seeing him even at a distance, but if she thought she had succeeded in discouraging him, she was mistaken. Lord Spendale had a good measure of his family's tenacity of purpose, and went ahead with his plans.

Thus it was that returning from an errand for her father one evening, when she had again unwisely not troubled to take a servant with her, she failed to notice a chaise and four standing outside one of the houses in the square. There was a groom at the horses' heads, a postilion astride one of the leaders. Eliane, deep in her own thoughts, paid no attention to so usual a sight, even though the vehicle stood in one of the darkest parts of the square. Flambeaux lighted other houses, but it was in a patch of darkness that she passed by the coach.

Suspecting nothing of what was to befall her, she nevertheless hurried on her way, not really liking to be out alone after dusk, even though so near her home, knowing that her father disapproved of her habit of walking alone. Suddenly the world became black and choking as a cloth was flung over her head, binding her arms close to her sides so that she could not struggle. A hand was clamped over her mouth, and she was picked up and bundled into the chaise.

Eliane fought and struggled like a wildcat, in utter terror. The carriage moved forward immediately and the horses gathered speed, amid warning shouts from the postilion. Miss Fielding went suddenly limp, and her abductor hastily freed her from the enveloping cloak.

The chaise traveled swiftly on, northward. At length, Eliane stirred and moaned. As she regained her senses a little, she realized that the cloak no longer muffled her, and that she could breathe as easily as her emotional distress would allow her, but the bumping swaying motion of the vehicle was brutal in its speed, and she felt sick, and moaned again. Then she opened her eyes. The interior of the coach was lit, the lamp flame flickering with their mad progress along the rough road, but the blinds were drawn. A voice she had come to hate said in her ear: "Do not scream, Miss Fielding, or I shall be compelled to gag you again."

She shut her eyes, thinking bitterly that she might have known who could behave so villainously. She opened them again, to see him lounging at his ease against the satin cushioned upholstery of the elegant vehicle. He was in a full dress suit of pale topaz satin and velvet, his dark hair powdered and tied behind in a black ribbon. The lace falls of his cravat and at the ends of his sleeves about his wrists were delicate and elegant in the extreme. He was undoubtedly a very attractive young man, and Eliane was quite sure that she loathed him.

It was true that she was a little relieved that her abductor was known to her, and not some further villain, but she was not ignorant of the world, and did not know what he might be capable of. She was still very frightened, but endeavored to hide it.

"Are there no depths to your infamy?" she demanded in a shaking voice.

"Certainly. I had no wish to murder you, so I have removed the gag, but I will replace it if you scream."

Her courage was at a low ebb. The swaying of the speeding chaise and her own apprehensions increased her feeling of nausea.

"Please take me home," she said faintly.

"In good time," he said. "Pray do not be too alarmed, Miss Fielding. You shall come to no harm.

If you wish it, I shall return you home in an hour or so."

She sat up abruptly. "I do not understand why you are doing this."

"You will not give me an opportunity to speak with you any other way. I have tried. You compel me to resort to such methods, though believe me, I had not intended to frighten you into a swoon."

"You are *too* good. All consideration!" breathed Miss Fielding, in valiant defiance.

His eyes gleamed appreciatively, liking her more and more. "Believe me," he said, "I realize I was mistaken at Vauxhall—although I cannot be entirely blamed seeing the company you were in! I have desired to make my apologies, but it is hard to get you to listen."

"Apologies! In this manner! I would rather be without them!" she cried angrily. "You are impossible!"

"That charge has been leveled before," he agreed.

"Insufferable!"

"That too," he said.

She struggled to appear calmer. "I do not accept any such apologies, but since you have now made them, will you please to direct your coachman to turn back!"

"After we have had supper."

"Supper! Oh, no, I will not. Where are you taking me?"

"To a house I own outside London. At Hampstead, to be precise. I repeat that you shall come to no harm, so rest easy, my sweet."

"I must return at once. Even now my father will be wondering at my absence. How can I explain to him?"

"Oh, doubtless we shall think of something," he said calmly.

"Abduction is probably a capital charge," she snapped, struggling against a feeling of physical helplessness.

"I will risk it. You see how much I adore you. Need it come to that, anyway?"

She knew that the last thing she wished was for her father to know that she had been subjected to this experience. Her temper flared in resentment against him. "Of course it is nothing to you, my lord, that you will cause my family distress. Have you any notion how utterly odious you are?"

"You grow monotonous, Miss Fielding," he said, and succeeded in rendering her speechless. She sat as far away from him as possible, rigid and silent, until her desire to be sick threatened to overcome her. For a seemingly endless time as the chaise jolted and swayed on its way, Eliane endured her discomfort as long as she could.

She pressed her hand to her mouth. "I—I feel unwell—I fear I shall be sick!"

He glanced at her white face, and lifted the blind a little to peer outside. "Hold on a while, Miss Fielding. We are nearly there. Would you like some brandy?"

She shook her head violently. She did not want him any nearer. She endured a further few minutes, and then, with a final swaying lurch, the chaise came to a halt. The servants jumped down and opened the door. Spendale glanced keenly at her, and then got out and turned to give her his hand.

"Come, Miss Fielding, you shall feel better inside. Let me assist you."

She looked at him, and then past him to the house,

which seemed to be a large villa standing in its own grounds. There were flambeaux giving a bright flickering light at the door, which was now open, revealing a well-lit hall and liveried servant in the doorway.

He saw the fear and question in her eyes.

"No—no—" she said.

"I give you my word," he said, and she allowed him to hand her down from the chaise.

Eliane was a little reassured by the presence of the servants, though she had no doubt that they would do his bidding only. She knew she was completely in his hands, but he had given her his word that she should come to no harm, and for the moment, she must believe him.

In the house, she waited until he had dismissed the waiting footman, and then not looking at him, said in a trembling voice: "Oh, why will you do this? I have done nothing to deserve it. You have made the most dreadful misjudgment—"

He took off his cape, and leading her into a room where supper was laid, and silver and glass sparkled in the light of the chandeliers, said in a matter-of-fact tone: "You will feel better directly, Miss Fielding. Let me offer you some wine. Then we shall have supper and talk a little. After that I will return you, as promised."

"I cannot eat," she said impatiently.

"I am sure you are not always so tedious." He dared to untie the ribbons of her hood, and taking it from her, drew her nearer the blazing fire. "Come, make the best of it, Miss Fielding. Let us simply enjoy a good supper and get to know each other better. There is no need for melodrama."

She flushed. "Melodrama! What else is such an

action as this—to bundle me into a chaise with a cloak over my head. To cause distress to my parents, who must wonder where I am. It is not melodrama if it is something *you* do, I suppose!"

She saw the laughter ripple across his face, and he raised a hand appreciatively. "Touché, Miss Fielding." He turned and pulled at the bell rope, and when the servant appeared, ordered that supper should be brought immediately.

Eliane tried desperately once more. "Will you *please* take me back?"

"I have said so. After supper."

She stared angrily at him, but he seemed immovable. She allowed him to assist her to a seat at the table. The food which began to appear was excellent, and she supposed with a feeling of astonishment that he must have planned this days before. He had learned of her movements and laid his plans accordingly. He was evidently efficient in his villainy.

Although she sipped her wine, she would not eat, but kept her eyes downcast.

After a moment, he said: "For pity's sake, Miss Fielding, the food is not drugged! I should not so insult my chef. Neither is there any laudanum in the wine you have taken. An excellent vintage, don't you think?"

She flashed him a look of pure dislike, and sipped her wine again, if only to quell this persistent feeling of nausea.

"If you will not try the soup, will you partake of some soles with oyster sauce? I am sure that Jacques has exerted himself tonight, and if you leave the food untouched he will surely abandon my service. You would not injure me thus?"

"I should like to do a great deal more," she said fiercely.

"Well, so you have done. You have slain me with the prettiest eyes I ever saw. Their dark blue is most unusual, and very, very beautiful."

He was rewarded by a flash from those dark blue eyes, but she said nothing as the servants entered. She would not give him any encouragement, but by now she would be having supper at home, and she was young and healthily hungry. She told herself that the faintness might lessen if she ate a little.

She paused. "If I eat, will you take me home?"

He sighed. "Shall I put it in writing?"

"Oh!" She felt an unaccustomed urge to violence, a wish to throw her wineglass at him, but preferred to keep her dignity. "Do you abduct females often?"

"Frequently," he said imperturbably.

"Oh." She might have known she could not disconcert him.

"Do you want to know about the others?"

"No—I—oh, how dare you? You are amusing yourself!"

"Of course."

Since she was not going to win this contest, she addressed herself to the food in silence. Spendale watched her. He was more and more puzzled about her. Her movements were graceful. If she disliked her situation, she did not appear to be intimidated or impressed by the elegance of her surroundings. She took her wine as if she were used to it. Her table manners were those of a lady.

"I do not understand you," he said at last. "How came you with those people at Vauxhall? They were plainly not your kind."

Eliane bit her lip. So he *had* judged her on Mrs.

Benson's behavior. Oh, ill-timed venture to rescue Ned!

"The young man was my brother," she said steadily. "The others—I was seeking to protect him from them, and did not realize I was exposing myself to a vile assault!"

His mouth twitched. "You are referring to that oaf from whom I rescued you, I presume?" His smile deepened as her breathing quickened. He said smoothly: "Your brother's name is Page. Your name is Fielding."

How did he know? "He is my half brother," she said.

"Not a blood relative, I think?"

"No. His mother married my father."

"And your name, besides Fielding?"

"Can be of no interest to you, my lord."

"Indeed, it is of the greatest interest. I know that it begins with an 'E.' Is it Ermintrude, Emma or Eve? The latter, I hope."

She did not reply.

"If you do not tell me, I shall be compelled to find out. It will not be difficult."

"Oh!" said Eliane once more. She did not want that. How he could get his own way, the wretch! "It is Eliane."

He repeated it after her, in some surprise. He gave it the same accurate French inflection that she did herself. He wondered if this might account for her seeming so different, but French blood in itself would not give her that undoubted air of breeding. "Your mother was French?"

Eliane did not answer directly. She had no wish to be questioned upon that youthful and long dead mother, for whose memory she cherished a fierce protective love. "Please, I do not wish to answer any more questions. You have promised to let me be."

Spendale took a thoughtful sip from his own glass. "I have promised to return you unharmed tonight. As for the rest," he paused, and held her eyes with his own, until her heartbeats quickened distressfully. "Can we go no further?" he said deliberately. "I have very much hoped so."

Even Miss Fielding could not mistake his meaning. Her chair scraped upon the parquet floor as she sprang back and turned away from the supper table. He was after her in a flash, towering over her as he had done at Vauxhall.

"Come, my sweet," he said softly. "Must you fight me so?"

She caught her breath. "This is an odious game you play to amuse yourself! You must believe your attentions unwelcome to me. Please, as you are a gentleman—"

"Oh, playhouse stuff!" he said lightly. "Are we on the boards at Drury Lane? I am but a mere man attracted to the prettiest of girls. I swear you have caught me completely. Can you not respond? Do you really so dislike me?"

"I—I loathe and despise you!"

He laughed. "Is that true? Or are you still indulging your taste for melodrama? Don't go too far. I might take you at your word. And that reminds me," he thrust a hand into his coat pockets, and drew out a slender jewel case. "This contains something of yours."

She took it, mystified. It was a handsome object, of fine leather tooled in gold, with a gold clasp. Fearing the worst, she opened it, and saw her own lace handkerchief which she had flung upon the ground at Vauxhall, now laundered to a snowy whiteness, but resting upon it lay an exquisite bracelet of delicate gold links and flowers of diamonds and small seed pearls.

"Oh!" She could not but admire his taste, even while she resented his intention. He came nearer, saying persuasively: "Come, sweetheart, yield a little and see how well we might fare together. I like you more and more, and I think you might come to like me very well. We might be very happy here. I would be generous—and faithful to you, I swear it—" His arms went around her gently, drawing her close, until she came out of her daze and drew back in a panic.

"Let me go! You promised! Are you a *liar* as well?"

She saw the hazel eyes flicker. She had succeeded in annoying him at last. Her own face was very pale as she laid the jewel case upon the table, but taking back her little handkerchief, she clutched it tightly in a trembling hand, and turned to face him, lashing him now with her only weapon, her tongue.

"Every syllable you utter, everything you do, only makes me detest you more and more. You say you have done this to apologize, but only to insult me further. What you offer may be acceptable to some poor females—since you must know those with whom you have succeeded, what makes you believe me to be the same? Is it anything *I* have done? There is nothing—nothing," she repeated with passionate indignation, "that I have done which could lead you to such a supposition! Only what you believe to be my circumstances, and your own *stupid* arrogance!"

Eliane had succeeded in shaking him at last. She expressed herself in words and phrases which did not belong to the kind of young woman he was used to amusing himself with. Her trembling rejection of him held a note of true outrage, and he felt he had persisted enough. To pursue a half willing quarry was one thing. To harass a frightened innocent was entirely another, least of all, in his code, a girl of the middle classes to whom her respectability meant so much. Viscount Spendale had undoubtedly earned a good deal of his regrettable reputation, until it had brought stern words from his father, but even for Spendale there was a line to be drawn in such matters, and he saw now that he had badly overstepped it.

What had he done? She hit back hard with her words "stupid arrogance." He thought now that he deserved them, and what she said was true. She had done nothing to make him rate her so low except for her ill-chosen company at Vauxhall. Since then she had consistently repulsed him with dignity. He had made a second error in supposing that he might persuade her to be his mistress. And the devil was in it that he liked her better than ever!

There was a tense silence as he stared hard at her, and then said slowly: "I see that I have indeed been stupid, Miss Fielding. I will not presume to offer you further apologies. You can be in no mood to accept them. Everything you can say of me I undoubtedly deserve."

He turned to pick up her cloak, thinking now only of returning the girl to her home without further delay, and to put an end to this episode as soon as possible. He looked down at her soberly, until her heart again missed a beat. "I admit and I very much regret my stupidity, Miss Fielding. It was unpardonable."

She did not know whether to trust this sudden

change of front and stood irresolute. Spendale continued to stare at her face, which had so unaccountably haunted him, and then said briefly: "We will return immediately, but first we must think of some story to satisfy your parents—for your sake," he added, "not mine."

He picked up the jewel case and replaced it in his pocket, turning to look at her again. "I have seen you bored, and angry, Miss Fielding, disdainful and—I sincerely regret it—frightened, but I have never seen you smile or laugh. I believe you could, and I regret that I may not see it."

She did not know what to make of him, but her eyes widened suddenly in consternation as there came the sound of horses' hooves and carriage wheels upon the graveled sweep outside. Spendale frowned and repressed an oath. They both waited in apprehension until he should have identified the sounds. In a matter of minutes, the gay, high voice of a girl came to him, giving instructions to the servants.

This time Spendale forgot Miss Fielding's presence and swore in earnest. As the girl's voice sounded nearer, he looked around, and then quickly motioned to the heavy curtains drawn in front of the window. "For heaven's sake, in there, Miss Fielding, if you please. This is my sister!"

CHAPTER THREE

The door opened only seconds after Eliane had moved hastily behind the curtains. Lady Ailsa swept in, dressed for traveling in a neat fitted habit of bottle green and a small silver-laced black tricorne hat with splendid plumes which curled down to her shoulder.

"*Spendale!* If this does not beat everything! It is the foulest trick. How do you come to be here? You were going to the Cleveden's rout!"

"So were you, I fancy! And what, Madam, do you here?"

"Well, I am in no mind to tell you. It is abominable. I felt sure this house was empty tonight, except for the servants. You said it was being let to some merchant's family next week. I don't know how you come to be here. It is most unfair!"

"I see I have upset you, Ailsa," he said tartly. "Your presence requires an explanation, and I will have it, if you please. Are you alone, and if so, why?

I cannot believe that you plan some sort of assignation?"

Behind the curtain, Eliane was amazed at the difference in his tone. What he did to amuse himself was one thing, it seemed, but he was elder brother to the Lady Ailsa Ardmore, and the chill authority in his voice would have daunted anyone else.

It did in fact have its effect upon Ailsa. She tilted her chin and prepared to defy him, but with Spendale looking so plaguey furious it required a little gathering of one's courage.

"Certainly not. Not the way you mean, Spendale. If you must know, I am to meet someone here, but we are eloping."

There was a stupefied silence. "Just like that?" said her brother at last. "May I ask who with?"

"Of course you may. It is Lieutenant Mackerras! Who else? I am utterly constant in my devotion to him."

"That half-pay officer I have heard you were fooling around with in Edinburgh! So much for Aunt Kirsty keeping an eye on you! He has followed you to London then. I don't doubt—if he's an honest man—who was the instigator of this!"

"Oh, you are horrid, Spendale. Is it my fault that Papa will not consider him? I am driven to this, by love."

"Fiddlesticks. And if you get what you deserve, you shall return home, and spend a month in the western tower at Glengarrick on bread and water!"

"You would not dare!" For all her romantic leanings, Lady Ailsa knew her Highland home and did not relish the incarceration threatened.

"When is this young fool coming here? I suppose I must run him through to teach him a lesson!"

"No!" Ailsa's shriek was genuine. "Spendale, you shall not!"

She glanced around the room, and her eyes took in the significance of the laden supper table, and the two settings with the unfinished meal.

"So!" she said triumphantly. "You are entertaining here yourself, Spendale, and since it is not at Park Lane, it is not a man, I'll declare. No wonder you are vexed at me! I see I have interrupted you, and am mighty inconvenient." She looked about her. "And who is it? I have interrupted your meal and you have hidden her! Well, I am sure that on second thoughts I don't wish to know. Your taste in females leaves a good deal to be desired!"

He made an exclamation, and Lady Ailsa's eyes sparkled, prepared to give fight. "Now you are annoyed! You think I don't know about these things? Pooh, I am not mealy-mouthed, and don't intend to be. But at least *I* am respectable, for Gavin and I plan to be married at Gretna, and then I shall face Papa if I have the courage. But you—!" She went off into a peal of laughter. "You are so angry, Spendale! Can it be someone interesting? Not one of your opera females? Some married lady perhaps? No respectable girl would be so mad as to sup with you here at Hampstead. You have hidden your frail out of consideration for me. How cross you must be, brother dear, that I have put you out of countenance!"

"Ailsa, if you are not quiet this instant, you will feel the flat of my hand," said Spendale between his teeth. "As for your plans for elopement, you will return to Town with me immediately. I will decide what to do with you—and with Mackerras later." He was furious with her. Miss Fielding must have overheard it all, and now he must get them both back to town. The prettiest situation! Was ever a man so plagued!

Miss Fielding had indeed heard all of what passed between brother and sister. A fine pair they were! Her cheeks burned at the humiliation of having to hide behind a curtain and hear herself so miscalled.

"I will not return with you," Lady Ailsa defied her brother, but without any conviction.

"You will do as you are bid, and since you must return in company with the lady I have here, I shall require you to treat her with respect, and to hold your tongue about the matter!"

"Ah, now, that I will not——" Lady Ailsa was quick to seize her advantage. The hazel eyes, so like his own, were sparkling with the zest of battle. "That I will *not* do. You cannot ask it! Travel back to Town with your—your creature! You must be mad. Really, Spendale, I had not thought it of you."

Eliane had heard all she intended to endure. The prospect of being compelled to travel back in company with the Lady Ailsa, who appeared to have all her brother's arrogance, was as unthinkable to Miss Fielding as it was to her ladyship. She looked around her desperately, deciding to make every effort to get away from this horrible house. Hampstead was not so very far away from London, and there must be a posting-house somewhere near from which she could get a conveyance of some sort to take her back to Soho. Cautiously she raised the sash of the window, thankful that the house appeared to be so well-maintained that the wood did not squeak as she did so. There was a short drop to the ground which she did not like very much, but she had no alternative. To stay and hear herself maligned was more than she would endure! She dropped as carefully as she could on to the paving outside, and gathering up her skirts, hurried out of the grounds of the house.

She paused briefly to take stock of her bearings. The house was upon a hill, and looking down the roadway she saw a glow in the sky which could only mean that London lay in that direction.... She hurried along the road. If necessary, she thought obstinately, she would walk all the way back to Soho, but stay in that house with that detestable brother and sister she would not!

In the dining room of the villa, the Lady Ailsa received the box on the ears with which she had been threatened. She was paying in part for the fact that Spendale was unaccustomedly angry with himself. In view of his changed opinion of Miss Fielding, the last thing he wished was that she should be forced to hide ignominiously behind a curtain and then hear herself further insulted.

He marched his sister out of the room, and locked her protesting in a closet until such time as he had attempted to make his peace with Miss Fielding. He went straight to the curtain, and drew it back, prepared to face her anger, but confronted only by an open window.

"Oh, the devil!" She was gone, and he knew she had been driven to it by what she had overheard. He cursed his own folly and his sister's tongue.

Released from her imprisonment, Lady Ailsa attempted to be adamant in her refusal to travel with her brother and his companion.

"Listen, Ailsa. You will do exactly as I ask, or I promise you I shall run your precious Mr. Mackerras through with as little compunction as I would a pig. The lady I had here did not deserve the remarks you were pleased to make, and in her distress she has run away, and is no doubt trying to make her way back to London. I must overtake her at once, and you will, I repeat, *will*, treat her with respect. Do you understand?"

"I hear you—" Ailsa's Scottish sarcasm implied her disbelief. "If she is what you say, then you must have been up to some trick, Spendale, which is no credit to you. No wonder you are angry with me! How like a man! It is yourself you should be angry with. Well, you shall not hurt Gavin. And I think I shall be interested to see this female. What is she? Some virtuous nobody you have tried to take advantage of," she remarked shrewdly. "What is her name?"

"Her name is Miss Fielding. And your diagnosis is roughly correct. You are a sight too forward yourself, Ailsa, and sadly lacking in the modesty which should be yours! I do not think our mother would care to hear you!"

Lady Ailsa's eyes flashed. His criticism was justified, she knew, and therefore all the more unwelcome, but coming from him...! She tilted her chin. "I think you would not care for either Mamma or Papa to know what *you* have done, Spendale. Do you think I do not know that Papa has been gravely displeased with you, and for what reason? Do you think that girls know nothing?"

"I think you know far too much!" he said with feeling. "Will you please now to hurry, and let us both endeavor to undo some of the harm we have done!"

At his tone, Lady Ailsa gave him a quick look, and surprisingly tiptoed to reach his face and give him a quick affectionate kiss. "Darling brother, you are really put out! You know, you are quite impossible, but then, we are a pair! How glad our parents must be that Neil and Meg are different." He had taken her arm and was hurrying her toward the chaise which had been brought around to the front of the house. "I am all agog to see your Miss Fielding. Is she very beautiful?"

He repressed a sigh. "She is," for so he now thought. "And I fear she will never forgive me." He assisted her to the chaise, and gave unblinking instructions to the servants to pursue the lady now fleeing across the wastes of the heath. His mouth tightened as the first heavy drops of a rainstorm fell about the chaise. As the vehicle gathered speed, so did the storm increase in intensity.

Lady Ailsa said unnecessarily: "She will be soaked. Poor girl!"

They had not gone far along the road crossing the heath when Spendale saw her and shouted to the coachman to stop. The rain was torrential, and she appeared to be trying to shelter beneath the branches of a huge oak. His lordship ripped off his cape and left it in the chaise for her use, and regardless of the ruin of his fine clothes, ran swiftly across the rough ground to where she stood against the trunk of the great tree.

Her dark curls were clinging damply to her face, her full skirts blown wetly against her figure in the boisterous wind. She was already shivering in the chill air.

"Miss Fielding! There was no need for this!"

She merely looked at him.

"Come, let me take you to the chaise. You are soaking wet already!"

It was a second or so before she could manage to

speak. "I will not come with you, nor travel with your sister."

"There is no alternative," he said impatiently. "I am sorry you heard what you did, but my sister knows enough now to treat you with respect. Please, Miss Fielding, do not waste time!"

As she remained still and mute, and he himself was getting wetter and wetter, he said angrily: "Confound you for an obstinate wench! Will you walk or shall I carry you?"

For a further moment she did not answer, but his annoyance was hard to bear. She held back a sob, and said flatly: "I cannot walk. I have injured my ankle."

He stared down at her in astonishment. "Yet you refuse to come with us? Do you imagine you are prepared to stay here on the heath in this downpour, thus injured? Pray do not be ridiculous!"

"I should obtain help somehow," she said defiantly. "Someone—some vehicle will come by! I will not go with you and Lady Ailsa!"

"Good grief! What are you made of?" For he recognized now a pride which matched his own, a courage which however misplaced, could not but command his respect. "Your innocence does you credit, but you are more like to meet a footpad, or worse! There are few who would travel across the heath unarmed! I am afraid you must steel yourself to endure my company, and that of my sister—"

Was it rain or defiant tears that now sparkled on the long lashes of those lovely eyes? As his glance held hers, angrily trying to compel her agreement, the anger was replaced by another, a far more momentous feeling. The biter was at last fairly bit. Alastair Ardmore, Viscount Spendale, the pursuer of pretty girls, knew himself in love. In that instant, when the breath seemed to go out of his body, he knew that this obstinate girl was going to mean all the world to him. Nevertheless, all he said was to repeat impatiently: "You must come with us!"

His sister's voice sounded above the rain, and he turned to see her preparing to descend from the chaise to offer her help. He shouted to her to stay where she was, and then, without more ado, picked up the unprotesting Miss Fielding and carried her over to the chaise. Brother and sister helped her in.

Lady Ailsa said matter-of-factly: "Let me take off your wet cloak, Miss Fielding. Spendale has at least left you his!"

The damp garment was removed and laid aside. Wrapped in his warm cape, Eliane allowed herself to look at the other girl, to find that she too was under polite observation. For her part, Eliane saw how alike were brother and sister, except that what was enchanting prettiness in Lady Ailsa was changed into masculine good looks in the brother. Eliane was prepared to dislike them both, but Lady Ailsa's friendliness was disarming. She returned her ladyship's interested look with all the dignity she could muster.

Any pressure upon her injured foot caused her pain she could not disguise. Spendale dropped on to one knee to the floor of the swaying chaise, and examined her ankle with great gentleness and unexpected expertise. Miss Fielding felt she might have been a horse, and was a little cheered to find her sense of humor not absolutely gone.

"I do not think there is a bone broken," he said. "But I cannot forgive myself."

"Nor I!" she said fiercely.

Lady Ailsa had watched the examination of the foot with a couple of swift glances under her long lashes at Miss Fielding's face. This young woman was a surprise. What had Spendale been at, to have such dealings with a girl who looked thus?

"I must apologize for my ill-considered remarks which you must have overheard, Miss Fielding," she said. "I have had my ears boxed, I assure you." She added with some acidity: "Spendale is a brute. I do not know what trick he played upon you, to prevail upon you to go to Hampstead, but it is time he was given a good set down. He gets his own way far too much."

His lordship bore this in silence. Eliane herself could not answer, could not make any comment upon this even had she felt it her province to do so. In spite of the enveloping warmth of his cape, she was beginning to shiver again. The rapid, swaying movement of the chaise was once more beginning to have its disastrous effect upon her. Her face became deathly. Then she felt her head being supported and a flask of spirits at her lips. "Drink this—" he said gently. She obeyed, and as the fiery warmth flooded through her, she opened her eyes, to look up into his contrite face. "I am sorry," he said softly.

To Eliane's distress, tears started to force their way to her eyes. She shut them tightly, concentrating hard on battling against this sign of weakness. Lady Ailsa said nothing to interrupt them but when Spendale resumed his seat on the other side of the chaise, she crossed and sat down beside Miss Fielding, and taking her unresisting hands, placed them in her own elegant fur muff.

His lordship appeared lost in thought. He had no alternative now but to treat Miss Fielding as the completely respectable young woman she undoubtedly was. This much he owed her, especially now that Ailsa had intervened in the matter so damnably. He said at last: "I have been thinking what is best to do. We may as well make the most of your escapade, Ailsa, now that you are here. We are obviously committed to a series of lies. I think we had best take Miss Fielding back to Park Lane—yes, Miss Fielding, pray do not begin to go against me. It will be better so. We may send word to your father tonight that you met with an accident and have been taken home by my sister. It will obviously be better if I appear in this as little as possible at the moment. Once your parents are reassured, Miss Fielding, your father may be sent for tomorrow morning to take you home. In this way, the length of your absence this evening may not pass unaccounted for. We may say you fainted, and it was some time before we knew of your address."

Lady Ailsa approved warmly, and Miss Fielding could only make her usual protest. "I would rather go straight home," she said.

"No doubt," he snapped. "But the damage has been done. You will allow that my proposal will raise fewer awkward questions?"

Reluctantly she agreed. It was the last thing she wished, to be taken to his home, an unwilling guest. Yet he was right. It was the best story to tell. She felt too ill to face any searching questions at home, and to have to tell her father what had really happened would raise a hideous scandal she could not endure.

Accordingly, when the chaise reached London, they turned toward Park Lane instead of Soho, and as the doors of the great mansion opened, Lord Spendale carried in like a bride the girl whom he had sought but an hour or so earlier to make his mistress. The irony of it occurred to none of them. Eliane was too dazed and apprehensive, his lordship too intent on making her comfortable, and the Lady Ailsa had suddenly remembered the note she had left for Lady Bray, announcing her elopement with Mr. Mackerras.

The housekeeper being sent for, she assured his lordship that there was a guest room ready immediately for the young lady. She also confirmed that Lady Bray had not yet returned to the house.

"Thank heaven for that!" said Ailsa, and flew up to her aunt's room to retrieve the note, still mercifully unopened. She dropped it hastily into the fire and returned to where her brother stood in the hall awaiting her before he carried Miss Fielding upstairs to her room.

"I will explain to Aunt Kirsty—it will serve to cover my absence from Lady Cleveden's, too," said Lady Ailsa, mounting the stairs beside her brother. "Then, Miss Fielding, we will send the message to your father without delay."

In the guest room, Miss Fielding was provided with some of Lady Ailsa's night attire, provided also with a wrapper and slippers, and was helped by her ladyship and her ladyship's maid Bridie into a bed which was far grander than anything Eliane could remember having slept in. The doctor was sent for, and at last Ailsa went downstairs again to find her brother in the library.

Spendale motioned to writing materials placed upon a table. "We will concoct this letter now, if you please, Ailsa, and you shall write it."

Eventually they came to some agreement upon its wording, and she wrote obediently:

> From the Lady Bray and the Lady Ailsa Ardmore to Mr. Charles Fielding at Dane Street, Soho Square.
>
> The Lady Ailsa Ardmore has the honor to inform Mr. Fielding that his daughter is at present resting at Ardmore House, Park Lane, after sustaining a slight injury from a passing coach. Apart from the injury to her foot, Miss Fielding is well and unharmed, and Lady Ailsa Ardmore begs the privilege of sending a coach to Dane Street tomorrow morning to conduct Mr. Fielding to his daughter.

"It will serve," said Spendale unenthusiastically. He folded the paper and sealed it with the Ardmore crest on his signet ring. "How did she seem, Ailsa?"

"As well as can be expected. I wish the doctor will not delay too long. If you want to know what she said to me, the answer is nothing—as regards yourself. I still cannot imagine how you prevailed upon her to go to Hampstead to be alone with you, and I will not ask, but really, Spendale, I had not thought it of you to make such a mistake. I gather her circumstances are not good—one would surely have met or heard of her—and there seems be no family but this father and a stepmother, but really, you should not treat respectable females so!"

"When I require a lecture on how to conduct myself, I will say so. In the meantime, are we to wonder what has become of the waiting Mr. Mackerras?"

"Oh, Gavin," she said cheerfully. "He will return to his lodgings, and await a message from me. He is amiability itself."

"He will need to be," said Spendale. His thoughts went back to the girl upstairs, and he was relieved when the doctor arrived.

This gentleman pronounced the injury to be a bad sprain, and advised poultices and rest. The young lady was obviously suffering from shock, he said. He departed having reassured them all, and when Aunt Kirsty returned from the Cleveden's rout, she found the absence of her niece and nephew from the gathering quite adequately explained, and promised to wait upon their guest the next morning.

The next morning, however, made it plain that Miss Fielding had taken a chill. Amid sneezes and a sore throat, her fever mounted rapidly, and Mr. Fielding, when he arrived, agreed that she should not yet be moved to Soho.

Eliane had spent a night feverishly wondering at the events which had overtaken her. She knew that her father had been told of her whereabouts and that he would come to collect her in the morning. She loved him dearly, and knew him for a quiet, unworldly scholar, protected from the hard economic facts of life by his capable second wife, but he was nevertheless no fool, and she wished she might feel more sure that he would accept without question the version of the evening's events which had been presented to him. How shrewdly, she wondered, might even her recluse of a father sum up the Viscount Spendale?

Trying at last to sleep, and having decided for her comfort that the two Ardmores had enough natural villainy to be able to tell a convincing tale, she felt grateful that whatever his detestable lordship's private activities, his family's household was impeccable in its respectability, and her father must surely feel this when he arrived the next day.

Had she been about the next morning, instead of battling with a rising temperature, Eliane would have seen that her abductor had no intention of absenting himself, and leaving explanations to his sister and aunt. On the contrary, he had every intention of meeting Mr. Fielding. Even Lady Ailsa thought he might well be abashed, but he showed no sign of being anything but the elder brother of the young lady who had found Mr. Fielding's daughter immediately after the accident. Whatever his inner feelings of embarrassment or remorse at meeting his victim's father, Spendale gave no hint. To Mr. Fielding he was agreeable, well-bred, and politeness itself.

To Spendale, Mr. Charles Fielding was a surprise. He had not consciously formed any idea of what her father would be like, but from the connection with the haberdasher's business in Soho, he had half expected someone who would match his idea of a tradesman. He was therefore unprepared to find her father a gentlemanly man, of scholarly appearance and speech. His clothes were faintly old-fashioned, as if he were indifferent to change, but they were sober and respectable as a professional man's would be. There was no attempt to put on finery which would have brought him into contempt.

Mr. Fielding gave Viscount Spendale the polite deference due to his rank, but no more than that. He was taken to his daughter's room, with Lady Ailsa hovering resourcefully in the background, and seemed, as indeed he was, completely unaware that the situation was anything other than as had been represented. Downstairs again, he thanked them all, paid his respects to Lady Bray, and departed for the day, reassured that he would be kept constantly informed of his daughter's progress.

For the rest of the day and those that followed, Eliane was left to recover in peace. Lady Ailsa's Aunt Kirsty visited her every day, but made no fuss. Lady Ailsa herself was busy with her own round of gaieties, but nevertheless she found time to visit the invalid frequently, regaling her with gossip with the same freedom she would have accorded anyone of her own world. Her comment to her brother was that "Pooh, anyone could have seen that she is a lady, even if her family are nobody in particular." She further fixed her brother with a warning eye, lest he should harbor any further designs against her. "I like her," she said.

"So do I," said his lordship with unrevealing face. He sent Eliane no direct message, much as he would have liked to do so, and repressed his first instinct to send her a basket of roses from the most expensive florist in town. He knew that for her sake it was better that he should do nothing to arouse Lady Bray's curiosity. He therefore resumed his own daily round, the nature of which would have surprised Eliane, who was ignorant of how busy young gentlemen of fashion could be.

He too rode in the park, sometimes at an early hour. He went to a fencing master's for practice with opponents worthy of his own skill. There was occasional boxing practice, a somewhat indifferent visit to a cockfight on which he wagered heavily, and a number of visits to gaming houses where he lost more than he cared to think about. Some of his other haunts saw him no more, which would have pleased his father. He also wrote his weekly letter to the Earl of Glengarrick, now traveling with his wife upon the continent. In a postscript to his mother, Spendale assured her that she need have no fear of her youngest daughter's behavior. He was keeping a watchful eye on her. Of Mr. Mackerras he said nothing....

CHAPTER FOUR

At the end of the week, when Lady Ailsa visited Miss Fielding's room, she found her very much better, and venturing to try her foot upon the floor.

"Well, to be sure, Miss Fielding, I suppose you must wish to return to your home, but I for one shall be sorry to lose you. Perhaps you could delay one more day, for tomorrow we are having a small supper party here, and I should like it exceedingly if you were to accompany us on your last evening."

"Oh," said Eliane uncertainly. It was very kind of them to ask her, always supposing that this invitation was not the result of some sudden whim on the part of Lady Ailsa, and unsupported by her brother or Lady Bray. Lady Bray had hitherto been unquestioning in her acceptance, having as Eliane suspected, been told nothing of her own humble circumstances, and Eliane did not wish to take advantage of her kindness. It would seem uncivil to refuse, and yet how could she endure to make one of a party which contained Lord Spendale? For a moment she hesitated, and then unwillingly agreed to the proposal, if Lady Bray should wish it.

"I think you are too tall for me to lend you one of my gowns," said Lady Ailsa speculatively. "No doubt you can send my maid to your home for one of your own?"

"Yes, indeed," said Eliane, thankfully aware of her last birthday present from her stepmother. It had been a really elegant dress of ivory watered silk, fully embroidered with scores of tiny posies. It was a lovely dress and would serve very well. She would not feel out of place in it, even in this great house. Swiftly she decided to ask her father to bring or entrust Ned with her mother's necklet for her to wear. It would give her courage to face the company at supper.

"Splendid, then that is settled. I do not know how many persons may come, but it will not be too many. Neil is back from Newmarket, by the way. You have not met my other brother yet." She laughed a little at Miss Fielding's expression. "Oh, you shall not worry! He does not resemble Spendale! Brothers were never more different. Neil is a true Ardmore, like Meg. Spendale and I favor Mamma." She chattered on. "I wish I had dark blue eyes like yours, Miss Fielding. They are so very pretty. Do you think people like opposites when they are in love? I adore Mr. Mackerras, and he is not like me at all. And Neil, it is a pity he likes Juliet Lawley so much. They both will be at supper tomorrow. I wish she were not coming. I don't much like her."

Miss Fielding knew this already, for Lady Ailsa had expressed her irritation with Miss Lawley before. "But Mr. Ardmore does?" she said.

"Oh, yes, and when Neil makes up his mind, it is

done for good and all. Except he has grown rather silent about it since she has seen fit to fling herself so much at Spendale! It is intolerable, the way she goes on!"

Miss Fielding was concentrating upon trying her foot upon the floor. She would not ask any questions regarding her tormentor, but her heart was beating faster, presumably because the very sound of his name could make her cheeks burn.

"That is splendid," said Lady Ailsa, watching Miss Fielding try a few unsupported steps across the room. "I think you should not try to walk far, though. I shall help you." She had sat upon the bed and kicked off her satin slippers, but now she thrust her feet into them again, and came to Miss Fielding's side, slipping one arm around her waist affectionately. "I shall miss our conversations," she said. "One cannot talk to Aunt Kirsty in the same way." She glanced up curiously at the delicate face which had attracted her disreputable brother. "Has Spendale sent any message at all, Miss Fielding? Or perhaps I should not ask?"

"None at all. Why should he?" Once again the treacherous color flooded her face.

"Well, considering that he has asked *me* every day how you did, I should have thought he would have sent you a message of some kind. He has caused you a great deal of inconvenience! No, please, Miss Fielding, we have avoided this subject until now. You must know that Spendale is well known to be a most tiresome rake. Indeed, Papa and Mamma do not approve of his ways, but that is not to be gone into! He has treated you very badly. He must surely wish to apologize to you, for he is not all bad, you know."

"I do not care for his apologies," stammered Miss

Fielding, with sudden foreboding. "Please—please say nothing to him to lead him to suppose I would wish it!"

"Oh, well, perhaps least said soonest mended, as Bridie says. You know, Miss Fielding," she added artlessly, "I have felt some curiosity about how he came to get you to sup with him at Hampstead. I suppose you would not tell me?"

"Certainly not," said Miss Fielding repressively. "It—it is best forgotten. There was a misunderstanding—"

Lady Ailsa abandoned her curiosity. "He is not wholly bad," she repeated. "Only pleasure-loving. Like me. Except that being a man, he may be as dissolute as he pleases, and few will really think the worse of him," she added practically. "Whereas for a female to do the slightest thing to lose her reputation is death!" She glanced at Eliane. "Is it not unfair?"

"It is the way of the world," said Eliane, feeling that the conversation had gone far enough. Her head was beginning to ache, and she did not wish to continue the topic. Lady Ailsa caught her tone, and saw that their guest's color had now ebbed to a greater shade of pallor. "You are tired," she said. "I have been talking for too long. I will leave you now. Good night, dear Miss Fielding."

The door closed behind her, and Miss Fielding, back in bed, lay with eyes closed. No, he had sent no message. She felt she did not wish for one. What she wished passionately was that she had never gone to Vauxhall that fatal evening. How much better to have abandoned Ned to the charms of Amelia Benson, and trusted to nature to disillusion him! The last few weeks had had their effect upon her. No longer accepting philosophically the situation in which she had grown up, her thoughts were for the first time running in the same direction as those of her practical-minded stepmother, when she wondered what the future held for the daughter of Charles Fielding? What could the future hold for her? That she could find endurable?

Miss Fielding buried her face in the soft down pillow, and tried not to think of that arrogant young man who had rated her worth only a dishonorable proposal. Suddenly, Miss Fielding felt unutterably forlorn....

The next day a message was dispatched to Soho to say that Eliane wished to return the day following, and making her requests regarding her dress and the necklet. Mr. Fielding sent both to her by the hand of Ned, who was, however, somewhat intimidated by the splendor of the Mayfair establishment of his sister's new friends, and having handed the bandbox to the footman, did not endeavor to see her.

Lady Ailsa's maid being entirely occupied with the problem of crimping her mistress's hair in the latest fashion, Lady Bray was kind enough to bid her own woman attend upon Miss Fielding. Eliane's dark curls were brushed until they shone and left unpowdered, piled high upon her head in the manner her father loved, and which left her delicate neck free to display the necklet. As she waited for Lady Ailsa to collect her from her room, Eliane fingered the jewels as they lay at her throat as if they had been a talisman.

There came a light tap upon the door, and Lady Ailsa swept in, her hair wide in the latest fashion, tied with a cerise ribbon threading through a riot of small curls. A cherry and white dress of deceptive simplicity rendered her so pretty a picture that Eliane exclaimed with pleasure. "How charming you look, Lady Ailsa!"

Ailsa looked critically at herself in Miss Fielding's glass and appeared highly satisfied with what she saw. "We are both very pretty, Miss Fielding," she said. "Is it not fortunate? And will you not simply call me Ailsa?"

"Oh, no, that would not be suitable," said Eliane firmly, feeling that any assumption of further intimacy with this family would never do. After tonight, she would be gone, and this whole episode would seem like a dream.

Lady Ailsa said no more, but slipped her arm through that of Eliane, and assisted her through the doorway and down to the next floor. Once more Eliane was conscious of the extreme elegance of the house and the wealth that must be the possession of the Earl of Glengarrick. No wonder, if his lordship were heir to all this and much more beside, he was so sure of himself, and so arrogantly certain that anything he desired he must have!

On the upper floor, the stairway branched to either side, but on the lower floor there was a large landing before the single flight to the hall. Lady Ailsa paused after their first descent, and opened a door, holding tight to Miss Fielding.

"Spendale wishes to speak with you a moment, Miss Fielding," she said hastily. "I think he wishes to make his peace with you."

Eliane cast one look to where he stood within the room, and turned to appeal to the departing Ailsa. "Oh, no, please, Lady Ailsa—please do not," but his sister had gone, and Miss Fielding was quite physically incapable of running after her.

Lord Spendale did not move beyond making her a deep bow. "You can hardly be expecting a repetition of my former behavior, Miss Fielding," he said.

"Oh, no, I do not." How like him to make even an apology sound like a challenge, she thought. She would not let him put her out of countenance so easily! "I do not know how much you have changed," she said.

He came across the room to where she stood, wondering how it was that every time he saw her she seemed more beautiful. As she stood there in her ivory silk dress, a necklet of some blue stones at her throat, he thought she graced his father's house as well as any woman he knew. Would she ever forgive him?

"Believe me, Miss Fielding, I did seek this opportunity to express my regrets, embarrassing though they may be to you—to both of us, perhaps. I could hardly have left them unsaid."

She was silent.

He went on: "I play this the only way I know, Miss Fielding. I assure you that I *am* utterly devastated at this unfortunate situation."

"Oh," said Eliane. She thought he still mocked her a little. "I do not believe you—that you have changed one bit!"

"Not in general," he said, with a faint ruefulness. "That might be too much to expect. But I assure you that toward *you* my attitude *has* changed!"

As she still could not answer, he said lightly: "Shall I go on my knees to ask your pardon? I will do so if it will convince you of my sincerity."

"You will make us both ridiculous if you do!" she said hastily.

"Well, then, could you not find it in you to forgive me—to trust me a little? Can we not appear friends, at least for this evening? I had hoped that your last evening here would lead you to think a little less hardly of me."

Such apparent humility made him seem so different, but she did not want to be disarmed. She needed all her defenses against his attractions. "My lord, I must thank you and your family for my care—"

Spendale stared down at her, as she hesitated for suitable words. As Lady Herrick had observed, Lord Spendale was not noted for obliging any but himself, but already his feelings for Miss Fielding were in a different category, and his thoughts were now tinged by an unwonted unselfishness. He recognized that his actions at Vauxhall and after had dealt a blow to her self-esteem which it had not deserved. His whole intent now was to salve that hurt, as much as he could.

He said gently: "We may resolve this unfortunate episode more easily, Miss Fielding, if you will not be too solemn."

He saw her head move, as if she were going to flash up at him an indignant response, but Eliane checked herself. He was right, of course. He was making what amends he could, in the most tactful way he could, and she must accept them, so that the whole affair might be put behind as speedily and completely as possible.

She bent her head in acknowledgment. He then bowed formally, and offered her his arm. "Shall we then join the company downstairs, Miss Fielding?"

She rested her hand lightly upon his arm, and they

walked toward the door. Eliane was experiencing an odd desire to cry, and did not wish to ask herself the reason. Tomorrow she would be gone!

Outside the door, they found Lady Ailsa waiting innocently by the window. She concealed her curiosity as to what had passed between them, and went immediately to the other side of Miss Fielding to help assist her down the stairs. Spendale now gave himself the pleasure of studying her bent head as she concentrated on her descent. The curls at her neck called for kissing as surely curls never had before, and then he realized with a stab of surprise that the sapphires she wore appeared to be real. He knew that Ailsa could have no such bauble to lend her. They must be her own, and how could one reconcile the possession of such a necklace with her modest circumstances as he had learned of them?

If Eliane felt his glance, she did not show it, except for a faintly heightened color. Spendale collected his thoughts and spoke suddenly to his sister.

"I should warn you, Ailsa, that you will find your Mr. Mackerras amongst our company this evening. I had meant to tell you earlier."

"Spendale!" Her voice rose to a high pitch of delight.

"Precisely. I warned you so that you should not shriek thus in the dining room!"

"But how? Oh, you are the worst tease! You were like Papa, I thought, and did not approve of him!"

"Hardly that, since I had not then met him. I made it my business to seek him in his lodgings. I liked him, so I have invited him to supper. But I have warned him that if he is to dance attendance upon you it shall be done properly. He knows that if he attempts any more clandestine marriage plans I shall dispatch him."

This was said so coolly that Miss Fielding had no trouble in believing that he would carry out such a threat, and for her own reasons held this also against him. Ailsa believed it too, and gave another shriek, but nevertheless skipped a little as they moved down the last sweep of stairs. "Dearest brother, I really do love you when I do not absolutely detest you. Miss Fielding," she added gaily, "confess that he has some merit!"

"I have not the pleasure of Mr. Mackerras' acquaintance," said Eliane sedately, and was rewarded by a chuckle above her head.

"You have your answer, Ailsa. You will not trap Miss Fielding into a kind word for me."

Already it seemed that the atmosphere was lighter. He was right to make it so, she thought again. They approached the drawing room, and found there assembled a larger company than Miss Fielding had anticipated. There was Lady Bray, as kindly and vague as ever, and a middle-aged lady of faded elegance and sharp, intelligent eyes, and a pretty young redhead, dressed in the height of fashion and a fine display of diamonds. These were Mrs. Ross and her charge, Miss Juliet Lawley. A tall, fair young man with a calm, handsome face was presented as Neil Ardmore. An elderly man in Holy Orders who looked as if he dined out more often than he prepared sermons, together with his wife and plain, clever-looking daughter, and lastly three young men. One was obviously Mr. Gavin Mackerras, from the way his eyes lit up at the sight of Lady Ailsa. He was a solid looking young man, considerably shorter than the two tall Ardmore brothers.

His manner was grave and everything he said was exceedingly correct. Eliane was amazed that this was her ladyship's adored Gavin, but swiftly concluded that perhaps Lady Ailsa's disposition would provide enough wildness for both of them, and that someone so obviously staid and sensible was in fact a very good choice.

The other two young men were undergraduates down from Cambridge, and were Mr. William Denby, younger brother of Lady Margaret's husband, and his college friend, Mr. Hugh Nash.

Eliane's curtsies were graceful and correct. Miss Lawley, magnificent in eau-de-nil satin, bent a sharp eye on the newcomer. Miss Fielding's gown of ivory watered silk with its delicate embroidered flowers was becoming, but quite unexceptional in her opinion. It was certainly not in the latest fashion, but she was pretty, and her sapphires were real enough. Miss Lawley had seen that fact sooner than had Lord Spendale. Who was she?

Miss Fielding's presence in the house was smoothly explained, and she was the subject of much sympathetic commiseration. The company all agreed that the traffic in London was beyond all bounds, that to traverse certain streets was to take one's life in one's hands. This topic having been exhausted before they moved into the dining room, Eliane was a little nervous of further questions, but she need not have worried. Lord Spendale had set himself to protect her.

Once they were seated at table, with Spendale at the head and Lady Bray at the far end of the long table, Eliane found that her former tormentor could be a well-bred host. She began to see a very different young man from the idle profligate he had hitherto seemed to her. He could, it seemed, be sensible and well-informed, and he guided the conversation deftly. It was in fact a merry company, and well chosen. The clergyman was a well-known wit, which accounted for his dining out six days a week. His wife and daughter were used to company, and while Mr. Mackerras said little, this was obviously his natural habit, and he cast no gloom upon the company. The two young men from Cambridge had intended to make their excuses after supper and to escape to more lively diversions, but with the unexpected presence of three very pretty girls and the generally gay and lighthearted atmosphere, they were happy to stay.

Lady Bray placidly enjoyed it all, and so to her surprise did Eliane. She remained graceful and dignified in spite of the one flaw in the evening, which was Miss Lawley's attempts to draw her out, attempts which were more than once deflected by Lord Spendale, at some cost to himself. Juliet was plainly willing to abandon anyone if she might have his lordship's attention. If there was a hint of displeasure in Neil Ardmore's eyes, she disregarded it. She was, as Mrs. Ross feared, determined to be brilliant, to outshine them all. Miss Fielding's quiet demeanor only stirred her to greater efforts to point the contrast, lest Lord Spendale see anything to admire in this new girl. She chose a momentary lull in the conversation to direct a question upon Miss Fielding's background, on her family's presence in London, and what her connection might be with their hosts. She thought that all three Ardmores seemed to have a greater regard for this Miss Fielding than rescue from a casual road accident would seem to justify.

Before Eliane could reply, Spendale leaned forward and said with an air of apology, which did not deceive even Juliet nor Mrs. Ross, who could have blushed for her, "I fear I did not explain, Miss Lawley. Miss Fielding's father and our own are acquaintances of long standing."

Eliane looked at his lordship with surprise. She had never expected to hear a more astounding statement, and could only think gratefully how kind it was of him to voice such an invention on her behalf. Spendale met her startled gaze with the faintest of smiles. "Mr. Fielding was only saying to me the other day," he went on, "that it is more than twenty years since he first met my father. It was in France, at the Château de Varency."

Eliane's feeling of gratitude and pleasure vanished abruptly. Watching her with interest, Neil Ardmore was suddenly reminded of a small defenseless animal hunted by predators. She had the same sudden air of stillness, of terror, and as if to confirm this surely fanciful supposition, the color ebbed dramatically from her charming face. He intervened tactfully, to give her time to recover her composure, if she were able. What lay behind her sudden distress he could not guess, but merely said in his calm way: "I was sorry to have missed seeing your father, Miss Fielding, but I was delayed at Newmarket."

She smiled gratefully at him, and was relieved when the Reverend Gabriel Webster was moved to remark that although he had never been in the neighborhood of the Château de Varency, he had spent many months traveling in France acting as bear-leader to the young son of the Duke of Sheildon. He proceeded to be very amusing on this subject, and attention was no longer focused upon Eliane.

She knew that Lord Spendale must have spoken the truth. He could not have invented or guessed at the name! This was worse to her than any statement she might have had to make to Miss Lawley about her modest home in Dane Street. It was so unlike her father to bring himself to mention her mother's family in France! However, as she forced herself to regain her poise, she felt she might trust that he had said nothing but that he had once met the Earl of Glengarrick.

Miss Lawley for her part now thought it advisable to turn her attention to Mr. Mackerras, winning his good opinion by her professed admiration for his regiment, and recalling others which had been stationed near her home in Virginia. She turned then to Neil, and having displeased him more than a little, had to exert herself to bring about his customary response. By the time dessert was upon the table, she had returned to her intended conquest of Spendale, sparring archly with him, seeking mock quarrels which he evaded, to the amusement of the company.

She was soon abetted by the worldly cleric, who had several good things in his repertoire on the subject of women and the notion of the ideal. Each guest was quizzed in turn, and the dining room rang with laughter in which Eliane found it impossible not to join. Spendale now permitted himself a more frequent glance at her. To see her smile and laugh was infinitely pleasing, and Juliet, catching such a glance, said jealously with intent to confuse her:

"Come, Miss Fielding, will you not give us your recipe for a happy marriage?"

The laughter died down to await her answer.

"I confess I have not thought about it greatly. I suppose—" she hesitated a little, but went on firmly:

"I suppose one essential is mutual respect."

Juliet was delighted. "Oh, how dull!" she exclaimed vivaciously. "What about love?" She immediately turned to his lordship, demanding that he should tell the company of the ideal woman he would wish to marry.

He looked at her with lazy mischief. "One does not necessarily marry one's ideal woman, Miss Lawley. Or wish to do so. It might even prove disastrous, to attempt to live up to perfection!"

"Oh, you shall not escape our questions! What sort of woman would you choose to marry?"

"I cannot be sure," he said. "I think upon reflection I should be wise to choose a docile mouse of a girl. One who was gentle and loving and utterly obedient to my every word, who would approve of everything I did, and who would never, never argue with me. Spirited females can be most fatiguing, I find."

Miss Lawley was not pleased, but it was said so blandly that even Eliane could not help smiling a little. Lady Ailsa was delighted at this set down for Juliet and clapped her hands. "Spendale is at least aware of his temperament!" she cried.

His lordship however chose to change the subject. The meal came to an end, and the ladies withdrew and left the gentlemen to their port. Spendale did not intend to prolong this, having no intention of depriving himself of any of the pleasure of Miss Fielding's company if he could help it. In the drawing room, instruments were sent for, and the sweet strains of the ladies' music soon lured the gentlemen from their wine.

Miss Lawley possessed a sweet and skillful soprano with which she was pleased to entertain the company. Miss Fielding proved a competent performer upon the harpsichord. The rectory ladies both played the violin, and Mr. Hugh Nash delighted the company with expertise upon the flute. The rest of the company joined in singing traditional and popular airs and amusing duets. The evening grew merrier and merrier, and Spendale fell deeper in love with every moment that passed. The magic of the evening was also upon Miss Fielding, who knew that the Viscount Spendale she was seeing here in his father's house was much more to her taste than the idle young man who had scandalously abducted her. Perhaps he was exerting himself to please, and certainly Mrs. Ross acknowledged herself surprised, but Eliane saw that in a different setting he could prove himself to be an able and indeed, rather clever young man. One, moreover, who could be kind when he wished, for he had protected her from the curiosity of his guests with a skill and kindliness which could only earn her gratitude and admiration.

It was already late when Lady Bray noticed that Miss Fielding's pallor was beginning to match the ivory of her dress.

"You are finding us a little tiring, perhaps, Miss Fielding, after your recent indisposition. Do not hesitate to retire, if you wish."

Eliane thanked her, and Aunt Kirsty rang the bell for her maid to be sent for, but Spendale came quickly to her side to see her to the foot of the stairs after she had bade good night to the company.

After she had gone, there was a buzz of approbation from those that remained. Mr. Webster pronounced her a truly delightful young woman, and his ladies generously agreed. Mr. Ardmore said calmly that they were indeed indebted to her for her charming company. Lady Ailsa said with more warmth than wisdom that she regarded Miss Fielding as her greatest friend.

At the foot of the stairs, Eliane hesitated, and glanced up at his lordship, catching her breath slightly as she met his eyes. The magic of the evening was still upon them both, and since they were alone, he was no longer bothering to conceal his feelings.

"Shall I carry you up? There is no one to see," he said with an affectionate smile.

It seemed to her that he spoke as if he accepted her as part of his own great world, but Eliane was not wholly bemused by the evening's enchantment, and said hastily:

"No—oh, no, I can manage perfectly—here is Lady Bray's maid to assist me. Good night, Lord Spendale."

He bowed formally, but added very softly: "Try to forgive me."

She could not reply, but began to mount the elegant staircase. She was not, however, in command of herself, and she caught the hem of her dress with her foot and stumbled with a tiny cry of pain. It was the very last thing she would have wished to happen, for he was, in a couple of long strides, beside her to assist.

"I shall carry you up! You are not fit," he said. "I am afraid this evening has tired you beyond your strength!"

Was this the same Lord Spendale who had callously abducted her and gagged her until she fainted? How he had changed!

A brief nod from his lordship dismissed the waiting servant. "See that Miss Fielding's room is ready, if you please," he said.

He gathered Eliane in his arms and carried her to

the upper flight. Miss Fielding said primly that she felt very foolish.

"There never was anyone more sensible," he said. They reached her door. In her room, Lady Bray's maid stood once more waiting, apparently deaf like the good servant she was.

"Will you—can you forgive me?" he said again. "You have not yet said that you do."

"Yes—oh, yes, but please let me go!" For the first time, her eyes deliberately sought and held his, and he knew that she meant more than merely setting her down on her feet. She was pleading with him that he would not seek to extend their acquaintance. He set her down gently, and bowed again.

"Good night, Miss Fielding."

He went downstairs to his guests. To let her go was what she asked, what prudence dictated, but not what his heart said. However, for the moment, and for the rest of the evening while his guests were there, he had to thrust her from his thoughts.

In a dream, Eliane submitted to being unlaced and undressed. Her hand went once more to touch the sapphires at her neck. They were all she had of her mother and her mother's world. In her long determination to be cool and unemotional, as others had not been, she had not allowed herself to be curious about that world across the Channel where her mother and father had fallen so disastrously in love. But now she was unsettled. Her stepmother and Ned—dear though they were—what part had they in this? Ardmore House, though but two miles distant, was a world away from Dane Street, Soho.

There was an ache in her heart which she was afraid to examine.

* * *

Downstairs, in the servants' hall, Lady Bray's maid showed that she was neither deaf nor dumb where her employers were concerned. She gave it as her opinion that his lordship, the young master, was fairly caught this time. The younger maids listened eagerly, but Leckie, his lordship's man, bade her sharply mind her own business. Leckie, so privy to his lordship's affairs as he was, might have his own views, but he did not consider it the province of anyone else to express an opinion.

Riding back in their coach to Portman Square, Mrs. Ross observed to Miss Lawley that Miss Fielding seemed a charming girl. Furthermore, she added, Lord Spendale had seemed very taken with her.

Miss Lawley did not agree. "He was polite to her, Ma'am, but no more. If you are meaning to warn me, I do not consider her a serious rival. I grant her looks are well enough, but she is plainly of no consequence, and that must weigh with him! If she were anybody at all, one would meet her!"

"You may do so in future, Juliet, if her father is indeed long acquainted with Glengarrick and his family."

"Well, then, she may do for Neil Ardmore. I intend to have Spendale."

"You make this a little too plain, if I may say so. And you may be overconfident, Juliet. I have not noticed him coming to heel. From what I have observed he does not intend to marry yet. He will take his time."

Juliet tossed her head impatiently. Mrs. Ross's gloomy prognostications were not at all to her taste. "You are forever dashing me, Ma'am," she said. "Depend upon it, I get what I want. It is my way."

"Then make sure, Juliet, that it is what you really want. I grant you Lord Spendale is an attractive young man, and he chose to be highly agreeable tonight, but he would never be an easy husband. Mr. Ardmore has the kindest disposition, and this in marriage may count for much. And since we must speak plainly, I would remind you that you would do well to weigh the fact that Mr. Neil Ardmore does not carry the same reputation for dissipation that his elder brother does!"

Juliet only set her pretty mouth obstinately. "I have a mind to be my lady," she said. "One may endure a few faults in a husband in order to be Countess of Glengarrick. As for Spendale's ill reputation—will he not leave that when he is married? And for his uneasy temper, I do not care a fig! We shall deal well enough together. He will mellow when he is in love!"

Mrs. Ross tapped her foot, shut her eyes, and said no more.

CHAPTER FIVE

Eliane was up early next morning. Now that she had made up her mind to leave, she could not go quickly enough. She made her toilette and bade the maid take her bandbox downstairs, and then visited the rooms of Lady Bray and Lady Ailsa to make her farewells. She guessed that his lordship had gone out riding and hoped to avoid seeing him. It was enough that she had formally thanked Lady Bray.

She sat in the morning room awaiting her father, passing the time with inattentive study of the *Ladies' Magazine* and the *Daily Gazette* and other papers which lay upon a side table. The door was ajar so that she might see her father when he was ushered into the hall, but the growing traffic of horses' hooves and carriage wheels outside left her unprepared for the sudden entry of Lord Spendale. He caught sight of the box in the hall, and looked quickly towards the morning room.

"Miss Fielding! Departing so early? Are you expecting your father so soon?"

"Yes—" She dropped him a curtsy as the head of the house in which she was a departing guest. "Good morning, my lord," she said formally. "I did ask that he should come early. I have said good-bye to your sister and to Lady Bray."

She found to her vexation that she was still a little afraid of him, still apt to be conscious of his first assessment of her and the deplorable action to which it had led him. She could never be quite easy with him, as she could with a certain Mr. Lionel Gretton, a young man whose approach was formal and whose manners toward herself had been impeccable. She could no longer complain of his lordship's manner, but she had been forced to an awareness of his masculine ruthlessness, and it left her uneasy. The supper party last night, she thought, where they had seemed so gay and upon such terms of equality, belonged to a dream which must vanish with the cold light of day.

Yet... as he stood there he looked so naturally elegant and handsome in his fashionable riding clothes that she could not feel the sensible detachment she wished to feel.

The silence between them seemed unnaturally long. She felt he must guess that she had tried to avoid seeing him this morning. But would he never say *something*?

Suddenly, Spendale realized that he was clutching his riding whip in a ridiculous manner, and flung it upon a chair.

"Eliane—"

She stiffened apprehensively, for he had never used her name before. Even on that awful night a week ago, at Hampstead, he had kept to "Miss Fielding." Surely, oh, surely he was not about to renew his former offer? Not *now*? Eliane felt sick—that she would not be able to endure the humiliation of it!

Spendale came closer, and looked at her searchingly. In the quiet of the park, he had wrestled with conflicting claims and painful indecision, but now he said abruptly: "Eliane, will you marry me? Give me an answer, and I will ask your father's permission as soon as you will—"

She caught her breath in amazement, and could make no reply.

"I have taken you by surprise. Well, forgive me, it has hardly been a courtship—I have not recommended myself—but there is all the future to tell you how much I love you—"

"Oh, no, you cannot!" she protested.

"But I can—and do," he said with a smile. "Do you think I do not know? I have loved you, I think, ever since Vauxhall, even though I did not know you then as I do now—love you and esteem you, Eliane—"

"No," she said faintly. It seemed as if a prospect of heaven had opened up before her, but it was a heaven she must resolutely reject.

"But it must be yes, Eliane. You must know my feelings. I started wrongly, and I shall never cease to regret it, but I soon realized my mistake. I love you—"

"Oh, no," she said yet again. "I could not—forgive me—I could never—"

"I have spoken too soon," he said anxiously. "You doubt my sincerity—it is not to be wondered at, but you must believe it."

"I tell you, I could not marry you! It is *unthinkable*!"

It was Spendale's turn to be astonished. He had not expected such an answer. He only knew that he had struggled with the realization that such a marriage would have his father's strongest opposition. It would certainly be universally regarded as a mésalliance. He had had to think hard about it. He knew himself very much in love, that he needed her if he were to mend his ways, and he had not thought her really indifferent to him. It had seemed to him, experienced as he was, that even from the start, when he had coolly amused himself teasing her at Vauxhall, that she had been aware of him. She had not been able to hide it. And not least, he knew he had so much to offer a girl in her position. As one of the most eligible men in society, he had not expected such a refusal from a girl of her humble circumstances as a passionate "unthinkable!"

He repeated the word after her, a quick surge of anger and pride within him. "Unthinkable? Do you mean that?"

He felt her scorn to be unacceptable. Surely they had progressed from his first error, or he would not have spoken. Had he not apologized again and again?

"Yes," said Eliane desperately. "Unthinkable. N-not to be thought of. I could never—never contemplate marriage with you."

He stared at her. "Eliane! For God's sake!"

"Oh, please do not persist!" She was almost tearful. "I cannot—could not marry you."

"Why not?" he demanded angrily. He saw that she did not wish to answer him, and felt she must be acting out of implacable resentment. But it was his whole future in the balance, and he had to make sure he understood her.

"You could not contemplate—could not endure to marry me?"

"No," she agreed miserably.

He continued to stare at her in blank disbelief. He had confidently expected a loving capitulation, an appreciation of what it meant to Viscount Spendale to make such an offer. He had anticipated with some pleasure the moment when he would feel her in his arms, for a kiss that would erase the memory of the very different one he had inflicted upon her at Vauxhall. Having made his decision, he had come back from the park with the eagerness of a confident lover. The contrast of his reception made the shock all the greater.

"Can I have mistaken your feelings?" he said. "I had thought that in spite of a bad start, there was a real regard growing between us. I chose to speak so early as this simply because of my former behavior. I wanted you to know how completely my regard for you had changed! Have I not made what amends I could? It seems that the offer of my name—my life—is not enough! You are not satisfied! I have liked your pride, but not this! You wish to humiliate me first as it lies in your power? Must you be so vengeful? Would you have me grovel in some further way, Madam?"

"Indeed, I would not!" she was stung into replying. "You are unjust. And if I say I do not wish to marry you, I do not expect to be raged at!"

He made an effort to collect himself, but could not forbear saying angrily: "In view of what I have offered you—what I would have you know I have never offered to any other woman before—your aversion to me must be great indeed!"

She turned away. Spendale made one more effort. "Eliane! For pity's sake let us not quarrel before we have even begun! Have I spoken too soon? Do you need time to consider? Eliane—I would wait—"

"Oh no—" She had to stop him, knowing that his arrogant temper would soon lead him to resent his humiliation, and that she must not make matters worse. "I have told you—there is no need to consider! I simply do not wish to marry you!"

Spendale's face had grown pale, his lips compressed. "Then, for the moment, there is no more to be said! I wish you every happiness, Miss Fielding. Your servant, Ma'am." He bowed and went quickly from the room, leaving Eliane with a face no less pale than his own. She had said what she must, and would not now retract a word of it, but she had not wished to see the hurt in his eyes.

She turned and wandered about the room, careless of and even welcoming the pain in her injured foot. She clasped and unclasped her hands, seeking to quell the turmoil within her. Marriage—to him! She stopped abruptly by the chair on which lay his riding crop. Her hand went tentatively to touch it where his hand had gripped it, and then dropped hastily to her side as the sound of heavy hackney coach wheels clattered outside, announcing the arrival of Mr. Fielding....

Spendale had mounted the stairs at a run of several at a time. On the upper floor he encountered Neil, also dressed for riding, who looked surprised at his brother's thunderous face.

"Ah, Neil—" His lordship's good manners did not desert him even in his rage. "Miss Fielding is downstairs, awaiting her father to take her home. Will you see them from the house for me?" He met his brother's eyes. "Confound all women!" he said savagely.

Neil's brows rose calmly. "All?" he said. But he asked no more questions, and went swiftly downstairs. Lord Spendale went to his room with a slam of the door which threatened to shake the whole house.

Upon Eliane's return home to Dane Street, it seemed that her accident and short illness had taken its toll of her. She greeted her stepmother as affectionately as ever, but had little to say of her experience, although she endeavored to oblige both Mrs. Fielding and Maria Taylor with descriptions of the splendors of Ardmore House. Mrs. Fielding was quick to notice that she seemed disinclined to go out of the house. Her motherly instincts were aroused, and she lost no time in acquainting Mr. Fielding with her views.

"The child is moping, I'll be bound. If she were not so sensible, I'd say that these society folk have turned her head. And that could not be wondered at, when all is said and done."

Charles Fielding admitted that he too had noticed his daughter's lack of spirits. "For this reason I have got tickets for the concert at Ranelagh tomorrow evening. I have invited young Gretton to join us. I know he enjoys music as you do not, my dear."

Mrs. Fielding was not affronted. She was tone deaf, and saw no reason to apologize for it. Her mind was on her stepdaughter's affairs. "Eliane likes Mr. Gretton, I am sure. He would be a very good match for her. Do you think anything may come of it?"

"Let us give the child time to choose," said her father with a smile. "But it could well be."

On being told of the concert at Ranelagh, Eliane's first impulse was to plead that she did not wish to go, since she knew that the gardens there were more frequented by the polite world than those at Vauxhall, and she did not wish to meet any of her new acquaintances there. However, she chided herself for her foolishness, and would not disappoint her father. That evening, she kept her fan instantly ready to shield her face, but her fears were needless. She saw nobody that she knew.

It was in fact the evening of Lady Tolhurst's ball, and it seemed to Lord Spendale that half London—his London at any rate—was there. He thought it an appalling crush, and said so acidly. It was not an occasion that either of the Ardmore brothers enjoyed, although their sister, having angled for and obtained an invitation for the unimportant Mr. Mackerras, was quite satisfied with her own evening. They returned to Park Lane together, and after bidding his sister good night, Spendale went into his brother's room.

Neil looked at him, and nodded dismissal to his man, proceeding to take off his cravat himself. Spendale watched him moodily, and then said abruptly: "What are we going to do about Juliet? Do you still want her?"

"I do—" Neil flung the neckcloth aside and began to undo the buttons of his fine lawn shirt. "And I shall get her, just as soon as she has tired of pursuing you. I may take it you don't intend to offer for her?"

"You certainly may. I thought that was understood. She bores me," he said disagreeably. "You must see something in her that I do not."

Neil's good-tempered mouth tightened just a little, but he would not be provoked. "I knew her before she came to London and met you. You have not seen her as she can be—as I know she really is. This success she has had in London has turned her head.

It is a phase she will get over. At least, I can only hope so. The real Juliet is different."

Spendale was unconvinced, but merely said: "No doubt you have the right of it, but it pleases neither of us that she should make such a cake of herself as she did tonight. I do not choose that she should think to give the town the notion that I have or am about to offer, but it is difficult to give her a set-down in public without offending you." He paused, and gave his brother a brief, affectionate smile. "I think you would do better if you were not so damned patient with her. Absence might make the heart grow fonder. Why don't you go up to Leicestershire? You have not seen our nephew yet! And Meg would be delighted."

Neil saw the point, but countered shrewdly: "Leaving you free to slap down Juliet without offending me?"

Spendale's gaze remained bland, but he thought ruefully that the close understanding between his brother and himself could have its drawbacks. He said smoothly: "I will undertake to send you an express should she be about to accept another man."

Neil did not answer for a moment. Then he gave a sigh. "I suppose I might. I am not doing very well here in town, and one of us should visit Meg. But have a care what you are about," he said warningly. He was lost in thought once more, and then said: "Shall I take Ailsa with me?"

"No, that's hardly necessary. I can keep a tab on her. And I have threatened her with the western tower if she oversteps the mark."

Neil laughed. "She'd have Mackerras scaling it with a rope ladder."

"I think not. But sometimes I think he's just the

sort of sobersides she needs. Perhaps we should be grateful."

He said good night abruptly to his brother and left.

Two days later Neil Ardmore set out for Leicestershire to stay with Lady Margaret and Mr. Thomas Denby.

Miss Juliet Lawley was a little surprised that the Hon. Neil Ardmore had left town without saying good-bye to her. She hoped a trifle uneasily that she had not offended him too much, but told herself that when one was in such great demand, he could not expect to enjoy much of her attention. If he had gone off to sulk, she was sorry, particularly as he had been singularly sweet tempered until now. She was therefore genuinely relieved to hear from the Lady Ailsa that he had merely gone to visit his twin sister, and to see her firstborn.

She also had a less admirable reason for regretting his departure. She had not scrupled to use him as a means of meeting his elder brother more often than she would have done otherwise. However, to her delight, it seemed that after Neil's departure his services were no longer necessary. To the surprise of Mrs. Ross and the mortification of Lady Herrick and others, Lord Spendale was seen to pay marked attention to Miss Lawley.

He had obviously come to heel at last, thought Juliet in triumph. So much for doubters like Mrs. Ross! And if his manner was still disconcerting, and she was never quite sure how to take him, well, that had always been his way. He had never been so easy a companion as his brother, but there was no doubt he was paying her all the attention she could wish.

He was frequently around at Portman Square on some pretext. He was invariably one of their party when they went out for the evening, at least for some of the time. It was not to be expected that he would give up gaming, but he had taken her to one or two of the more respectable houses where the play was excitingly deep. It also seemed that when he could he brought his sister with him, and Juliet, taking this to mean that she was soon to be one of the family, did her best to be highly agreeable to that young lady.

Lord Spendale was, of course, merely pursuing a scheme to please himself. He was above all awaiting a suitable opportunity to further his courtship of Miss Fielding, but in the meantime, he had a notion to advance his brother's cause by sickening Miss Lawley of himself by some highly capricious behavior. His insistence that Ailsa should accompany them so often was partly that she should be witness of it and also that he might in turn keep watch on her, as he had promised his father he would do. Such machinations pleased his sardonic sense of humor, and he did not think that Miss Fielding was likely to hear of his attentions to Miss Lawley.

Lady Herrick was furious, and told her son that he might now consign his hopes to the devil. It looked like being a match, she said, and she viewed his lordship when she met him with no liking. Her feelings were shared by other mothers whose sons desired Miss Lawley's fortune and person, and mothers whose daughters sighed in vain for Lord Glengarrick's heir.

Lady Ailsa spoke of it to her faithful lieutenant during one of their unobtrusive meetings in the park.

"I have never been so astounded in my life, Gavin,"

she said, linking her arm confidentially with his. "I could have declared that he had no interest in her. And what of Neil? It is too provoking. But at least Spendale is more agreeable when he is with her, so I suppose he has come to like her a good deal. He is certainly a different being at home. *There* his moods are past all bearing, and he may bite one's head off twenty times a day!"

The Lady Ailsa was in fact still a little sore from the dressing down his lordship had given her on the matter of a card debt she had had to confess to him. It had been unfortunately high, she admitted, but it was not that he or Papa could not afford to get her out of a little difficulty. Admittedly it was not the first she had incurred, but who would have thought, since everyone wagered and gamed a little or much, that it would have brought down upon her head an acid lecture on what card games she might play, at whose house she might play them, and to what extent she should control her stakes?

"Really, Ailsa, can you not keep out of trouble for two days at a time?" Spendale had said irritably. "Playing cards with Charlotte Mayo and her brother, or people like Elsworth or Major Pickering is not for young ladies straight out of the nursery. You had better stay at home playing snap with Aunt Kirsty. But tonight, you shall come to the play with me." He added with an expression she could not read. "You will be company for Juliet."

Even at the play, which was amusing and had them all laughing in the most agreeable manner, Ailsa found that she transgressed again. She suddenly caught sight of her dear Miss Fielding in another box at the other side of the playhouse, and delightedly drew Spendale's attention to the fact.

Miss Fielding was looking positively ravishing, although with persons unknown and not of the first elegance. There was Mr. Fielding, and a lady whom she did not know, and very much in attendance upon Eliane was a young man of distinctly personable appearance who, as Spendale instantly saw, was not the brother whom he had seen at Vauxhall.

His lordship had never before known the tortures of jealousy, but as he saw her turn her lovely head and speak and smile to this young man, he knew them now. When he had told her after she rejected him that there was, for the moment, no more to be said, Miss Fielding had taken this for a mere figure of speech, but she underrated his tenacity. He did not intend to let her go. That evening, however, he turned a deaf ear to Ailsa's suggestion that he might like to invite Mr. Fielding's party to join them for supper. To Eliane, sitting at the far side of the theater, it seemed that he never at any time looked her way. His attention was all for Miss Lawley.

Bored with the cooing of that lady and her brother's surprising response, Lady Ailsa slipped out of the box during an interval and went around to Miss Fielding's party to renew her acquaintance. She was greeted with great courtesy by Mr. Fielding, and with grave deference by Eliane's younger companion. She came blithely back to her own party with the news that Miss Fielding was well, that the young man was an amiable creature called Mr. Gretton, son of Sir Lewis Gretton the brewer, who was himself reading law at Gray's Inn. She also came back to a glowering look from her brother.

Ailsa's mouth puckered a little, and after a while, she said she had a headache. Juliet at once suggested that immediately after the play they might take her home to Park Lane, and that Lord Spendale might then come back to Portman Square for supper with herself and Mrs. Ross.

The evening was not without significant consequences for any of them. Lady Ailsa surprisingly sobbed into her pillow that night. Her passionate affection for her elder brother was never in any way diminished by any contest of will between them, but of late, Spendale had been hard to bear. She now sobbed that Alastair was utterly hateful, that Juliet Lawley had bewitched him, and that Neil would never forgive him his treachery.

Furthermore, said the Lady Ailsa to herself, she would marry her darling Gavin the moment she could persuade him to ask her. She wished that Mamma were nearby with her gentle counsel, and that Papa were not so set against Lieutenant Mackerras. To be sure he was poor, but so were most Scottish lairds. It was the Ardmore family who were unusual in their capacity for marrying heiresses.

To Miss Lawley it seemed that the Earl of Glengarrick's heir was about to offer for a certain heiress himself, and she waited confidently for his declaration. Her spirits and her radiant looks were commented upon. Mrs. Ross, that shrewd woman who did her conscientious best to guide her charge through the rocks and shoals of London society, hoped that she was not due for a disappointment. She had made it her business to be more aware of Lord Spendale's reputation as uncertain, willful and worse. Whether the raffish company he chose to be seen with so often was no worse than that indulged in by many another gay young rake, and whether or not he would settle down irreproachably after marriage was not for her to guess at. All Mrs. Ross knew was that she would have been much happier had Juliet chosen his lordship's brother, who while he would have no title did undoubtedly have a much pleasanter disposition, and be less likely to dissipate Miss Lawley's fortune.

To Mr. Charles Fielding it seemed that his happy thought to invite Mr. Lionel Gretton to be one of their party had not been entirely successful. He was beginning to realize with a good deal of misgiving that all was not well with his daughter.

As for Miss Fielding herself, if she had not fully known before where her heart lay, she knew now. Precisely when Lord Spendale had ceased to be detestable and when he had become someone to dream about she did not know. She had no thought to marry him because she knew—who better?—the pitfalls, the misery that a misalliance could bring. But to see him at the playhouse and have her presence ignored.... Eliane found it difficult to be sensible and tell herself that this was precisely what she wished.

CHAPTER SIX

The London season for the Polite World continued merrily on its way, while ordinary London clattered and roared about its business. In his chambers at Gray's Inn, Mr. Lionel Gretton pursued his studies doggedly, interrupted by pleasant reveries regarding Mr. Fielding's daughter. Mrs. Fielding carried on her haberdashery business in the shop which served so well to provide for her family. She too knew of the existence of the sapphire necklace, but never to her excellent mind had there been any question of expecting her husband to sell it to enlarge their way of life. They lived comfortably enough, and she had no wish to interfere in matters which she considered were beyond her. Ned seemed to be settling down to fixing his attentions on Maria Taylor. She even thought there might be an early marriage there, with a closer association between the two shops. Suspecting the existence of Mrs. Amelia Benson and ladies of her kind, Mrs. Fielding thought with relief that Ned was a good boy, and the spit and image of his father.

If Mr. Charles Fielding seemed a little more abstracted than ever, what was to be made of that?

At Park Lane, matters were going less well, though not sufficiently obviously for Aunt Kirsty to notice anything. Lady Ailsa's days were more than full. Lady Bray exerted herself to go shopping with her niece, spending happy hours choosing hats, dress materials, ribbons and laces, poring over designs and fashions, buying gifts. There were visits to the circulating library, for in her quieter hours the widowed Lady Bray enjoyed a good long novel, but Ailsa read little in London. That was for the long months at Glengarrick Castle. London was for gaiety. With all this activity, visits to friends and visits received, as well as picnics, boating parties and other delights, Lady Ailsa had difficulty enough to steal moments alone with Mr. Mackerras when he could get away from his regiment, now quartered near Colchester. She slipped out of the house to meet him in the park, sometimes taking her maid with her and sometimes going alone. When she told her brother that she loved Gavin Mackerras "to distraction" she spoke the truth. She intended to marry him, and she needed a confidante. Miss Fielding seemed to exist providentially to fulfill such a role.

Thus when Eliane returned from church one Sunday morning she found herself greeted by a young lady stepping from a sedan chair.

"Miss Fielding! How pleasant to see you!" The chair was dismissed, and the Lady Ailsa linked her arm through Eliane's with persuasive friendliness. "Let us walk back to your home. I'm sure we have so much to talk of—"

Bridie the maid was bidden to follow and they walked back to Dane Street. By the time they reached the Fielding home above the shop which said "Mrs. Mary Page—Haberdashery" Lady Ailsa had accepted Miss Fielding's invitation to enter for some refreshment. Bridie was to be entertained downstairs, not at all averse to a good gossip with Molly and the other servants in this household which was so unlike Ardmore House. The gossip however was but brief, for Bridie was dispatched back to Park Lane with a message for Lady Bray that her ladyship was staying for Sunday dinner with Miss Fielding in Dane Street.

Lady Ailsa being at ease in all company, enjoyed herself very much. Mr. Fielding she knew already, Mrs. Fielding was in her opinion a very good sort of woman, and if Ned Page were alternately dumbstruck and self-assertive, well, Lady Ailsa had had this effect upon young men before.

Mr. Gretton joined them for the meal, and she was again quick to observe his adoring attitude toward Miss Fielding. After dinner, Miss Fielding and the Lady Ailsa had the modest sitting room to themselves, and her ladyship settled herself comfortably, prepared to unburden herself.

"Now we can talk, Eliane. I have vastly enjoyed myself, but you—you are not like your family! Spendale said you were not."

Eliane's expression caused his sister to say hastily, for fear she had offended, "But then, they are not your family, are they? Except your Papa, of course."

"They *are* my family," said Miss Fielding. "And I love them dearly. Not by blood, I know, but by all the ties of years of affection and gratitude. As for being different," she added more lightly. "Are you not all different in your family?"

"Not in the same way." Lady Ailsa was ever candid. "And to be sure, sometimes we are too much alike. Was ever such a pair as Spendale and me?"

"How are your ladyship's brothers?" asked Eliane quickly.

"Oh, I daresay Neil is well enough. He is in Leicestershire, you know, with my sister Meg. He writes that the baby is dismally plain but improving. Well, Thomas Denby is none so ill-looking himself, so no doubt the child will improve. Neil says he is likely to stay up there a while. He and Tom deal famously together, but I sometimes think Neil has absented himself deliberately because he does not care to see Spendale so much with Miss Lawley!"

Miss Fielding wished to deflect the conversation to other topics, but for the life of her could not. Lady Ailsa Ardmore brooded darkly. "As for that wretch Spendale, of course he is well! When was he ever ill? But provoking in the extreme."

She got up from the sofa where they both sat, and peered at herself in the gilt looking glass upon the wall, and then walked restlessly about the room.

"You can have no notion how he has changed!" she said with a slight sniff. "I wanted to come to London to be with him because I thought we would have a famous time with Papa and Mamma away on the Continent. But he has grown so prim and proper, at least where *I* am concerned. I don't understand him, Eliane. He and Miss Lawley are forever in each other's company—the whole town is talking and expecting an announcement in the *Gazette* any day. Yet half the time he insists that I accompany them! It is utterly boring, though I must say Miss Lawley is all amiability to me. Sometimes I even like her! Spendale seems agreeable enough when she is there, but oh—the difference at home! I suppose he has decided he wants her for himself, but is not happy at the thought of what it must mean to Neil!"

Eliane forced herself to say with a faint smile: "It is difficult to envisage Lord Spendale being prim and proper."

Lady Ailsa paused in her perambulations and laughed. "Indeed, it is a change for him, but I suppose he promised Papa that I would not see too much of Gavin. Nor do I wish to upset Spendale in this, for he would call him out as soon as not. And though I don't know about Gavin—he is too sensible to be a fire-eater—I do know that Spendale is a deadly shot, and goes to the Fencing Academy to fence with the best." She sighed again. "I wish he had not chosen Juliet. Neil will not like it."

Eliane at last succeeded in changing the subject, and then the gentlemen returned. Lady Ailsa however thought it time she returned to Park Lane, and it was arranged that a coach should be called, and that Miss Fielding and Mr. Gretton should go with her.

Ailsa bade them good-bye outside Ardmore House, and skipped in happily to meet her brother in the hall.

"You have had your dinner," he said shortly.

"Thank you, yes," said Ailsa, realizing that this was his way of saying that he had been advised of where she had been. "And I enjoyed myself very much. More than I would have done playing gooseberry to you and Juliet."

To her surprise, he laughed. "Does that bear hardly upon you?"

Ailsa stared at him. "Oh, Alastair, for the moment, you looked—more like yourself." In spite of herself, her voice quavered childishly.

He had the grace to look ashamed. "Have I been such a brute lately, puss? If so, I'm sorry. I've been bedeviled—"

She moved closer to him, looking up at him with eyes so like his own. "I haven't understood you," she said. "We never bickered so before. Is it because you are uneasy—I suppose you *must* have Juliet, in spite of Neil! I admit she is very pretty. I told Eliane that the town has been expecting an announcement in the *Gazette* this last sennight!"

"The devil you did! I see you have been busy, Ailsa!"

"There now! What can I have said that is wrong? Have you not made it plain to all the world that you intend to have Miss Lawley?"

His Lordship looked exceedingly put out, but he said nothing more beyond reminding her that they were having company that evening, and would she please to guard her tongue from now on?

Lady Ailsa closed her eyes. She felt she needed the quiet matter-of-fact support of Mr. Mackerras, whose stolid temper, so unlike her own, could always be relied upon. If his regiment went overseas, as he seemed to think, how would she bear it?

Mr. Lionel Gretton with great correctness first asked Mr. Fielding's permission to approach Eliane. Mr. Fielding gave it willingly enough, since Mr. Gretton bore an exemplary character and would undoubtedly make his name at the bar. He would also inherit a fair fortune from his father. Charles Fielding felt that his daughter could safely be left to make her own decision on such a matter. He was also not sorry that she should receive such a good offer, but he expressed no surprise or disapproval when Eliane gently rejected the young man. Mr. Gretton was much dashed, but signified that he was prepared to wait and ask again. He continued to visit the house in Dane Street with no suggestion of embarrassment, for which Miss Fielding was grateful.

She thought she might never see Lord Spendale again, unless it were at a distance, as she had that evening at the playhouse. She accepted that she knew very little of the pattern of life of the Ardmore family. They were likely to travel a good deal, and to spend months on their estates in Scotland. The difference between their aristocratic way of living and her own modest if comfortable existence in Soho was inescapable. Their worlds lay apart.

However, the Viscount Spendale did not plan to leave London for a while. He had his sister to watch over, and he was much occupied in escorting Miss Lawley whenever she wished. He was on his way to the Fencing Academy in Piccadilly with Sir George Rayner when he saw Miss Fielding and her father enter Drummonds' the booksellers, and he instantly persuaded that young gentleman to change their plans.

Eliane was examining a book when she became aware of the two elegant young men. It was obvious to Spendale that he had startled her, since she was unable to suppress her feelings. It did not seem to him that it was dislike that he had seen in her eyes.

He bowed, and came toward her, remarking easily upon the pleasure it was to see her, and begging leave to present his companion. Sir George professed himself enchanted, wondering to himself how it was that that devil Spendale always managed to find the prettiest girls. And how about the forthcoming nuptials with Miss Lawley? He sincerely hoped that matrimony would not sober his friend, a dismal consequence he had seen far too often!

Mr. Fielding detached himself from his business with the bookseller and came to greet his lordship, but presently he proposed to go, having completed his purchases. Spendale took leave of the understanding baronet, and begged permission to accompany Mr. Fielding and his daughter. Together they walked through the busy streets toward Soho. To Eliane it was a secret, unlooked for happiness. The sound of his voice, with its faint Scottish intonation, a quick glance at him from beneath the brim of her wide straw hat, and she could have wished the distance twice as long. She would have been happy to have said nothing, wishing only to hear him speak with her father, but Mr. Fielding had taken pleasure and pains with the education of his daughter, and would not suffer her to remain silent.

They parted in Soho Square. Lord Spendale's manner to her had been impeccably correct and formal, and she felt once more that this must be the last time she would ever see him. That mad episode which had begun in Vauxhall Gardens was now ended, and they would go their separate ways.

In this she was mistaken. Spendale could endure to wait no longer. The pleasure of seeing her so unexpectedly made nonsense of his desire to be patient. Swiftly he decided that the time had come to put an end to the foolery with Miss Lawley, who would, he hoped, be sufficiently incensed to come to prefer his brother.

Eliane was wholly unprepared for his further visit

the next day. She returned from an errand to find Molly on the alert for her return.

"Miss Eliane, the master has asked that you will join him, to pour tea." She seemed excited, and Miss Fielding gave her a second look. "There is another gentleman with him Miss, so the mistress has ordered the best silver to be used. I have taken in the tray already."

Eliane hurriedly changed her gown and went to join her father and his visitor, whom she supposed to be one of his literary cronies, but as she entered the room, it was Lord Spendale who turned toward her and made her a low bow. He looked very grand in claret superfine with silver buttons and buckles. The embroidery of his waistcoat and the exquisite falls of Mechlin lace at his neck and wrists were such as made her very much aware of her own plain gray-silk, so suitable as it was for Dane Street.

"Lord Spendale! I had thought to find my father here—" she stammered, completely taken aback.

"He has gone to fetch a book we were discussing," said Spendale, but his eyes held hers. He added frankly: "He may take his time about it, Eliane. I have sought and obtained his permission to speak to you."

"Papa! Oh, no, how could he? He surely would not!"

He did not think to fail a second time, and smiled with good-humored amusement. " Perhaps your father does not regard my pretensions as unfavorably as you would seem to do!"

She could not smile in return. She could not credit that her father had given him permission to ask her hand, since surely he of all men would know that such a marriage could only bring regret to his lordship and humiliation to herself? Once again she was distressed to wonder at her parent. Had he taken Lord Spendale into his confidence? She gazed in trepidation at Spendale's handsome face, trying to read in it whether her fears were justified. Yet they could not be, or this interview would not be taking place!

"What—what did my father say?"

"What should he have said? Only that he gave me permission to approach you once more, and that he would never control your choice."

He moved nearer, saying pleadingly: "Surely the fact that I have come again pleads my cause? I misjudged you once, but I knew even as we stood in the rain on the heath that night that I would love you. I need you—as a wife." He paused, and then went on: "I have cared nothing what reputation I bear amongst the gossips, but I regret it now if it will divide us. I swear that what is past in my life is past, if you will have me!" As he looked down at her, waiting for her to speak, he knew that he would regret the activities of the past few weeks, if she should learn of them, and as he recalled Ailsa's account of her visit to Dane Street, he said hurriedly: "I trust you will believe me, whatever you may hear! Tell me, Eliane, is marriage to me still *unthinkable*?"

She turned her attention to the tea tray. The best silver teapot was heavy, and needed both her slender hands to hold it. Then she set it down again, as if she did not know what she was doing. "Lord Spendale, when I used that word, I did not intend to offend you so. I deeply regret doing so, but my feelings are the same. I do not wish to marry you."

She spoke coldly because she dared not let herself be swayed. To hint that she felt the distance between them too great would serve little. He could hardly be unaware of this aspect of the matter himself, and if he chose to disregard it now and override any arguments she might make, his regret would surely come later!

As she remained silent, he said sharply: "Is it someone else you care for? Is it Lionel Gretton?" He did not believe it, but wished to hear her deny it. Still she said nothing, and he said quickly: "This is indeed something I had not thought of, so sure was I that you were for me! Your father did not warn me!"

"No—oh, no—you go too fast, my lord!" She flushed a little, and pretended to be annoyed. "Must you marry me off to *someone*? May I not make up my own mind?"

"Indeed you shall," he said smiling. "But I shall hope to persuade you! Will you at least reassure me that I am forgiven for that sorry error—or must I wear sackcloth and ashes for ever more?"

"Oh, no—yes—" she stammered breathlessly, anxious to reassure him on that point at least. "I declare I have no wish to remember it at all!"

"Well, then, shall it be understood that in future we deal on equal terms?"

"Lord Spendale," she said desperately. "We cannot deal in future! And as for equal terms—"

She immediately regretted her words, for he took her up swiftly. "So now! At last I may guess the reason for your refusal! You fear the difference in our situation? Is that what holds you back—makes you rebuff me?"

She said steadily: "If it were the only reason, it would be quite enough."

"I must disagree. If I ask you to be my wife, is it

not plain that I am satisfied we should be happy together?"

She twisted her hands. "No—no—we should never suit. We should quarrel interminably. Your—your temper is too swift and overbearing!"

"I should endeavor to mend it," he said. "As you might perhaps contrive to be less obdurate over every matter!"

"There, you see! We should be ever bickering! I will not be persuaded against my better judgment! Why will you persist so, my lord? You must allow me to say no!"

"You say it frequently, Miss Fielding."

She had forgotten how those swift rejoinders could take the wind out of her sails. He was still the Viscount Spendale who had abducted her and teased her, still incalculable. He surprised her yet again, for he was looking down at her with an expression which made her heart beat faster.

"I cannot let you go, Eliane. I must—must believe that you will come to care for me—"

She held fast to her resolution, but said desperately: "I pray you will excuse me now. I—I will seek my father," and with some loss of dignity was already at the door before he could reach it to turn the handle for her.

She shut it swiftly behind her, and then went to her father's small study. Mr. Fielding looked up from his search among his bookshelves to give her a considering glance.

"Papa! I beg you to excuse me—I will send Molly to pour your tea." She could not forbear to voice her surprise. "You gave your permission to Lord Spendale, but you must know that I could not contemplate such a marriage, Papa!"

"I thought you should at least receive his offer, child. I thought he deserved that, at least. I am sorry if you were caused any distress."

"But you must know it would never serve!"

"If you are thinking of his character, Eliane, I believe him to be more sound than he is given credit for—"

"Forgive me," she said agitatedly. "I do not wish to discuss it, Papa. You—you will go to him, now?"

Her father smiled. "I will soften the blow for him as best I can. But, Eliane my dear, do not distress yourself! Young men recover from these disappointments in time."

This observation was not wholly successful in raising Miss Fielding's spirits. As her father prepared to go to her rejected suitor, she said hesitantly: "Papa, you were once acquainted with the Earl of Glengarrick. Are they—the Earl and Countess—very proud and grand?"

"They are a proud family, child. It is an ancient title, with wide connections."

She said no more. This was all the answer she needed. How soon, she wondered, before Lord Spendale recovered from his disappointment? She pondered upon his lordship's ways. "Whatever you may hear," he had said. Was this to be taken as a reference to his attentions—indeed, his apparent pursuit of Miss Juliet Lawley? His own sister surely could not be mistaken! Would he change his mind now, and seek to marry Juliet, who was so much better placed, in the world's opinion, than Miss Eliane Fielding? She hoped that if such an announcement reached the *Gazette* she would not have to read it.

* * *

The Viscount Spendale took his second rejection hard, but not in either way Miss Fielding feared. He neither flung himself into an orgy of dissipation, as he might once have done, nor rushed to propose to Miss Lawley. Indeed, the offices of the *London Gazette* received no such notification as the town awaited, and Juliet knew at last that there would be none. The congratulatory atmosphere which had surrounded Mrs. Ross and her charge now subtly and rapidly changed to one of malicious sympathy. Instead of offering for Miss Lawley, Lord Spendale was seen to withdraw from his pursuit, even to the extent of paying noticeable attention to one of her rivals.

In the morning room of the house in Portman Square, Juliet suffered an uncomfortable and plain speaking review of her position from her chaperone and mentor. Mrs. Ross could contain herself no longer.

"To be sure," she said with feeling, "I never thought he would! I dare swear he had only been amusing himself. Heaven knows you have made it easy enough for him, Juliet! Now he has turned to the Adamson chit! Men do not like to be hunted, and in spite of all my warnings, you have flaunted your hopes to the world! You have only yourself to thank. What your father would say I do not care to think! And yet I have done my best for you." She brooded indignantly upon Juliet's failings and Lord Spendale's perfidy. "I would not even put it past him to have been repaying you for your treatment of his brother," she added, more near to the truth than she realized. "The Ardmores have ever stuck like glue to each other's interest. After all, they are Scots, and clannish, however much time they care to spend in town. I should have been happy—very happy—to see you choose Neil Ardmore, but now he has taken himself off, the Lord knows where! I cannot blame him. You have not dealt fairly with him!"

"He has gone to Leicestershire to see his sister. She is his twin, and has but lately had her first child." Juliet roused herself to answer this tirade. She was, however, saved from further scoldings by the entry of a servant to announce that Captain Warnham of the *Savannah* had arrived below, and was asking to see them.

"Oh, show Captain Warnham in here, Belton," said Juliet eagerly. That the *Savannah* had anchored meant letters from home, and Juliet was feeling more than a little homesick. It was one thing to be the reigning belle of the London season when all was going merrily, but quite another to know defeat and have one's defeat known to all the Polite World. As the elderly captain was shown in, she gave him her hand delightedly. He was an old friend of the family, and there would be news that would warm her heart, even if she could not in return send back the gratifying announcement that she was to become the Viscountess Spendale and future Countess of Glengarrick.

Captain Warnham was an agreeable visitor. He produced letters for both ladies and stayed a while, but informed them that while his vessel lay off Deptford, he was taking the opportunity to visit his sister in Birmingham, and expected to be out of London for a week.

While he was there the atmosphere lightened a little, but with his departure, Mrs. Ross reverted to the problem of her charge's future. "It may be that we can save our faces a little, if we leave town," she said. "After all, you have not seen Bath, and if we spend some time there the matter may die down. If Lord Spendale cares to follow, so much the better, but I'll warrant he will do no such thing."

Juliet had been reading her father's letter. She listened with half her attention to Mrs. Ross, who finding her charge made no response to her suggestions, regarded her with some exasperation. At last Juliet looked up. Before Captain Warnham's visit she had wanted nothing better than to pack her bags and leave town, even to returning across the Atlantic, but now, as she stared at her father's letter, and then back again at Mrs. Ross, the courage and tenacity which had made her father and grandfather carve position and fortune from the virgin lands of America came back to sustain her. She was Juliet Lawley, and she would not easily admit defeat! Her eyes glittered as she regarded Mrs. Ross.

"Bath? We will see. Now, if you will excuse me, Ma'am, I have letters to write. Pray make my excuses to Lady Herrick and Mrs. Pomeroy if you are returning their calls this morning—"

She went to her room. She heard Mrs. Ross depart in the carriage to make her morning calls, and then sat for a good half hour at her escritoire, tickling her enchanting nose with the tip of her quill pen, and catching her underlip thoughtfully as she stared ahead of her. Then she wrote a number of letters. When at last she rang the bell to summon the servant to take them to the post, there was a sparkle in her green eyes which boded ill for someone.

Lady Ailsa came back from morning visits to find her brother in the library of Ardmore House, also writing letters. She wasted no time in giving her news and views.

"Spendale, it is quite tiresome how people are forever gossiping about you and Juliet. There are now rumors that she is to remove to Bath. Were you quarreling the other night?"

Spendale said indifferently: "I doubt if we were quarreling, not more than usual."

"But are you going to marry her?"

"No."

"She cannot have rejected you! You mean you have not offered?"

"No."

"And don't intend to?"

"No."

"Then," said the Lady Ailsa, drawing a deep indignant breath, "I take leave to tell you, Alastair, that you have treated her intolerably. You must admit you have encouraged her of late. I did not think you could be so selfish—even you! First you trick Miss Fielding, and try to seduce her! And then—"

"Ailsa, have a care!" he said sharply.

She ignored him. "Well, did you not? My dearest Eliane! I know you realized your mistake, but how could you have been so stupid as not to see from the first—"

"Be quiet! And you may leave Miss Fielding out of your homilies, my baby sister!"

"All right then, but I assure you Mr. Lionel Gretton made no such error! He plainly worships her, and I don't doubt she will be very happy to have him. As for Juliet, this I cannot understand! You have sought to amuse yourself and hurt Neil to no purpose! How could you? You are a devil!"

"Oh, have done!" He took a step toward her, his face indeed satanic, and the Lady Ailsa took a hasty step backward.

"Oh, aye, you'd box my ears again!"

He checked his anger, and turned back to his writing. He dipped his quill into the ink and then looked up at her. "Aunt Kirsty was asking for you," he said coldly.

Ailsa stared at him, and then swept out of the room.

Spendale took a fresh sheet of paper, and then began to write to his brother. There was news to be sent that their parents were now on the return route of their lengthy tour. The date of their return was uncertain. He was glad to know that Meg and Tom and infant were well. He might himself come down later for the hunting....

He paused, debating whether to say anything of Juliet. He thought of Ailsa's news. Even he had to admit that his behavior of late had been brutal. Was Juliet hauling down her colors and fleeing to Bath? If so, it might prove better for Neil to travel direct to Bath from Leicestershire. He wished them well!

His quill flew over the paper in his firm decisive script.

> ...As for Juliet, I have laboured villainously on your behalf, but I think she may now come to appreciate you a little more. No doubt the Town thinks worse of me than ever, but you know how much I care for that. Treat her gently—she may have had a rough passage of late—I know you will, and I wish you happy—

He paused, and then opened the drawer of the desk and put in the uncompleted letter. Better, he thought, to make certain of Juliet's moves before he wrote. Tomorrow would serve for that. He sat there a while longer, his thoughts no longer on his brother's affairs, but on his own. He had had no idea that the oft-sung pains of unrequited love could be such a shattering experience when actually undergone oneself. His idea of love had until now been a matter of gay pursuit and sensual pleasure. This ever present hunger for the wife he wanted was a fierce and painful experience. He knew that Ailsa's complaint that he had become hard to live with was justified. He locked the drawer of the desk thoughtfully and then went up to his sister's room.

She greeted him watchfully, still disapproving, but having so deep an affection for him that she could not bear to see the unhappiness she sensed in him.

"I thought we might call upon Smart the miniaturist," he said. "It is your birthday soon. Would you like your portrait done, puss?"

She was delighted, instantly responding to so agreeable an overture of peace. She tiptoed to kiss him, demanded how soon they should go to Mr. Smart, and silently promised the resulting miniature to her darling Gavin to take with him on his duties abroad.

The next day, arrangements were made with Mr. Smart for Lady Ailsa to sit for her portrait. Spendale then took her amiably enough on a round of calls, but declined to accompany his sister and aunt to Lady Clentwood's ball that evening. Instead, he took himself off for an evening's gaming. It was late in the evening when he left the house and made his way to Mahon's, off St. James's. He walked swiftly, taking for granted the London life as it was lived around him. Carriages of all kinds, solitary riders, sedan chairs, hackney coaches, strollers and revelers, sober citizens about their lawful occasions, women of the town and beggars importuning for alms—he gave them little thought. He was feeling restless, and his suggestion to Neil that he might go to Leicestershire for the hunting had not been an idle one. He was even thinking of Glengarrick. He was in fact getting tired of London, and would have made one of his sudden journeys had it not been for Ailsa's presence and his promise to his parents.

London also held Eliane, and it was not easy to remove oneself from the city where she lived, even though he reflected morosely that she might as well be in outer Mongolia for all that he might see of her. His decision to spend yet another evening at the tables arose mainly from the satisfying need to concentrate when he played cards.

As he crossed the road to Mahon's, he noticed a pressgang proceeding along the street, and felt some surprise. Such a collection of bullies did not usually operate at the better end of the town. The navy must be desperately short of men! He turned into Mahon's elegant establishment and went to the room where several games of faro were in progress. He proceeded to win and lose, lose and win in such a fashion as might have warned him of the unsettled state of his luck.

It was very late indeed when he left Mahon's, several hundred pounds the poorer, and decided perversely to try his luck at Dowding's, where the play was customarily even deeper.

The tables at Dowding's were full, but Viscount Spendale was known to play deep, and several of his acquaintances offered to make room for him. He sat there an hour, getting a run of neither good fortune nor bad, and then suddenly laughed in self-mockery, and throwing down his cards at the end of the game, decided to go. It was raining as he left, but he declined to take a chair. Once more he walked swiftly through the streets, now much emptier of people, and made his way toward the Strand. Down a narrow alley he stiffened suddenly to see his way blocked by the same pressgang he had seen earlier. Irritably he called for passageway, but they did not make way for him as he expected.

With a feeling of incredulity that they should think to assault such as himself, his hand went swiftly to his sword hilt. He caught sight of their officer, no more than a stripling, and shouted to him to haul his bullies off. Spendale's blade whirled defensively as it was plain that they meant to get him. He shouted again to the young officer, but as the men rushed him, he received a blow on the head from behind and knew no more.

Lord Spendale came to consciousness with a head that throbbed painfully, and for a moment that was all he knew. He was lying upon something soft and reasonably comfortable—a bed?—but then as he shifted painfully and groaned he realized that he could not move his hands. They were tied with cord. Then he became very alert, aware of the gentle rise and fall of a ship at anchor and the creaking of timbers around him. Before he opened his eyes he remembered the pressgang. The world had gone mad when some midshipman thought to press the Viscount Spendale upon one of His Majesty's ships!

He opened his eyes at last, and focused them with difficulty upon the face and bulk of a giant in seaman's rig. Spendale remembered him, a hulking great brute. He proceeded to express himself in very clear terms.

The sailor would not have thought it from the foppish clothes. He listened with respect, and then interrupted: "Best stow it, cully. Ladyship present."

His lordship turned his head swiftly and immediately winced at the pain of his protesting head wound. He stared with utter incredulity at Miss Juliet Lawley, whose face had reddened at his language, and who now said: "Oh, thank Heaven—I did not mean you to be hurt—not so much."

She hurriedly dismissed the huge sailor, bidding him take guard outside the door of the cabin.

Spendale regarded her thoughtfully. "Miss Lawley's private pressgang! I had thought the world had gone mad when people of rank were to be pressed, but it is only Miss Lawley that has gone mad!"

How like him to recover his self-command instantly! There was a steeliness about him which never failed to attract her even while it could frighten. And she was frightened now at the enormity of her behavior, no longer looking forward to telling him what she had done. "I am sorry for your head injury," she said again. "I did not intend—I assure you—"

"You did not intend your sailors to split my skull. But why this absurdity, Miss Lawley?"

She drew in her breath, attempting to match steel with steel. "You have thought to make a mock of me, Lord Spendale. You have amused yourself—and half London—in leading me to suppose that you would ask me to marry you. Then when it pleased you, you have made it plain that you do not so intend. Well, then, I have shown you that I am not to be trifled with. I have a little more spirit!"

"So!" He looked surprised, but his eyes were watchful. "I am knocked senseless and carried on board a ship. One of your father's, I presume? Are you sufficiently revenged, or is there more to come?"

"Yes," she said, as a daring new idea came to her. "You shall stay here until you *do* marry me!"

He stared at her for a moment, and then began to laugh a little. "Oh, upon honor, Juliet, I swear I never liked you so well. To think that I was finding London dull!"

She flushed. "You may mock. You think I am a brash, untutored Colonial, not up to the ways of your English 'polite world'—"

The laughter died from his eyes. He liked her better for standing up to him. Perhaps Neil's taste was not so much awry after all. But she would have to learn there were things she might not do. "Must I remind you that you have sought to make it plain to that world that *you* intended to have *me*? Let us speak plainly at last, Miss Lawley. I had thought only to teach you a lesson. You rejected my brother, and I did not care to be placed in a false position by your persistence. I will choose my own wife. You have only yourself to blame—"

"I could hate you," she said with feeling. "But you *shall* marry me!"

"With my hands tied, no doubt. And a split head?"

She came back toward him and with unaccustomed fingers managed to untie the knots of the cord. "I have said I am sorry for that—and I am—"

"You cannot play these games with a chicken-skin fan. Seamen are rough creatures who use cudgels. Did nobody warn you? You have stepped into a man's world, Miss Lawley. Most unmaidenly of you."

He smiled maddeningly at her angry response. "I will not ask if the captain of this vessel knows of this?" He glanced about him. "A fine ship. So we must assume he does not. You must wish to keep your method of obtaining a husband as secret as possible." He put up a hand to his head. "It throbs like the devil. How did you prevail upon that beardless youth to commit this outrage? I'll have his blood—"

"No," she said quickly. "He is not to blame. I told him you had done me an injury, and that this was a way of teaching you a lesson. You must not blame him—he is very young."

"And doubtless highly impressionable. And your seamen hit harder than you realized."

"I have wanted to *kill* you!"

"No doubt. I have vexed you a good deal. But rest easy, my sweet. I have no intention of making you my wife, and I think that upon reflection you might be glad of it. I should make you the devil of a husband. I suggest you have me put ashore as soon as you will, and let us put an end to this farce."

His conscience pricked him. He had not thought to drive her to such lengths, but only into the arms of his brother. He had not thought it the happiest way to begin a marriage, but he had been sure that if she accepted Neil, she must come to care for him speedily enough.

Juliet remained obstinate. "The captain is absent, but shall marry us when he returns. I have accounted to the mate for your presence. We said we were showing a gentleman around the ship when he fell down a companionway and injured his head. You must not think I entered into this lightly—"

"I think you entered into it when your wits went woolgathering." he said bluntly. "You have it all planned most comically, Juliet, even to your bully outside the door, but for one thing. Nothing in the world would lead me to marry you. What compulsion you think to apply, I cannot imagine. Perhaps you threaten to murder me?"

"If need be," she said defiantly. "The sailors would do my bidding."

It was of course the merest fantasy. She had intended no more than to keep him prisoner while the notice of their betrothal appeared in the *London Gazette*, to be followed by a second notice to say that the arranged marriage would not now take place. Thus the Polite World would believe that Lord Spendale had offered and been accepted and then jilted. They would laugh at him for a change! She thought he would never dare reveal the truth, lest the town laugh the more.

But she had not the courage to tell him this, yet. She guessed shrewdly that he might laugh at threats of murder, but his response to her impertinence over the announcement in the *Gazette* might be another matter. She had no knowledge of the importance of Miss Fielding, but she was now afraid of the consequences of the affront to his male pride. One never knew what his reaction would be!

Yet she could not bear to admit defeat. So many men had wanted her, even a Duke, although her stomach might turn at the thought of being united to such an old roué as the Duke of Sheildon. There had been Neil Ardmore. Why must this one other man she wanted prove so impervious to her attractions? She must try once more to win him, so that her confession about the announcement would become a mere jest between lovers.

Lovers.... Juliet swallowed hard. "You—you *have* liked me," she said.

"As a prospective sister-in-law. Never as a wife. You are a fool, my girl. You should have taken my brother while you had the chance. He is worth four of me, and you've not had the wit to see it."

Part of her—that shrewd, sensible Juliet which London's vanities had obscured—knew he was right, but she did not want to think of Neil. She still wanted to triumph over Spendale, still aimed at becoming the future Countess of Glengarrick, and to snap her fingers at all those shallow, insincere people in London whom she secretly despised. Not least, she still believed herself in love with him.

She forced herself to meet his eyes. He wondered where her thoughts had been.

"Well, Miss Lawley?" he said evenly. "Do you summon your bullies and your baby-boy officer and have me put ashore?"

"No—" she panted. She added, as coolly as she could: "Will you give me your word not to try to escape, if I leave you untied? You will be more comfortable, and it will be less embarrassing."

This caused him to hoot with derisive laughter. "By all means let us avoid embarrassment! As for escape, you have not told me what vessel this is, nor where it lies. We are at anchor, and in a river. Possibly an estuary. Somewhere in the Thames, I suppose, and anchored nicely midstream. What am I supposed to do—swim?" Deliberately he sounded amazed, intending to conceal from her that if forced to do so, he would do just that. He was not certain how determined a jailer she might be, but he had no intention of remaining her prisoner. "I cannot see your minions allowing me to get to a boat," he said.

"No, they would not," she agreed eagerly. "You *are* my prisoner." She came closer to him, her eyes now searching his face, trying to stir him out of his insulting indifference. "Alastair," she used his name hesitantly. In her gown of soft yellow silk, in the dim light of the cabin, she had never looked prettier, softer or more yielding. If she could get what she wanted, she was his for the taking, and for the moment, she had the satisfaction of knowing that a brief flame flickered between them. "Can't you love me?" she whispered.

He looked down at her. "Apparently not," he said deliberately.

She reddened, knowing that she had cheapened herself in his eyes, but she was not wholly dissatisfied. She might still win. She moved away and walked toward the door of the cabin, turning back to look at him once more. His expression was unreadable. "I will send someone to look after you, and bring your dinner," she said. "Think it over."

She left him to his thoughts, which were not the ones she hoped for. She gave instructions to the big seaman not to let the prisoner out of his sight, but to wait upon him, and went to her cabin. Lord Spendale must eat alone. She had to dine and charm the youth who had done her bidding at the cost of his career on Captain Warnham's ship.

In the passenger cabin, Spendale lay more at his ease. His head wound still throbbed, and he thought it would be a day or so before it mended sufficiently not to bother him. He owed Juliet and her little midshipman one for that. His handsome face wore a thoughtful smile. It occurred to him that Juliet's time must run out. She had doubtless counted upon a quick victory, on being able to present him as her future husband. She must grow increasingly embarrassed as the days went by with no such assurance, but only the problem of explaining the continued presence of her prisoner to the captain of this vessel. She had got herself into a tangle, and his lordship did not think he would help her out of it.

His smile deepened. He had begun to like her a little more now. Her genuine indignation at his behavior was very much at variance with the artificial airs and graces with which she had sought to snare him. He was no longer so bored with her, and he thought he would be in no hurry, after all, to seek his release. He would sit it out and see what Juliet would make of that. Before they had ended this farce, Neil's foolish love would be cured of her infatuation for Viscount Spendale! In the meantime, he thought that a message, suitably vague in content, might be dispatched to Lady Bray, to remind her that she was for the moment solely responsible for her niece.

The gentle movement of the ship did not trouble him. He stared at the ceiling of the cabin, and thought of Eliane....

CHAPTER SEVEN

Lady Ailsa had returned from Lady Clentwood's ball in company with Lady Bray, and on being informed that his lordship had not yet returned, remembered that he had gone gaming and was not likely to return before the small hours. Declaring herself to be exhausted by so many parties and balls within a week, she had gone to bed and slept late. It was gone noon the next day when Bridie brought in her hot chocolate together with the day's newspapers for her ladyship to while away the time until she should think of getting up.

Lady Ailsa sipped her chocolate sleepily, and looked casually over the day's news. She was not interested in the speeches of Mr. Burke in the House of Commons, or the fact that the York Stage had been attacked on Finchley Common, or that two shops had been burned down in Fetter Lane, less still that a number of malefactors had met their fate at Tyburn gallows. She turned over the pages of the *Gazette* to glance at the latest gossip, lest she should have missed anything of note at Lady Clentwood's. It would never do not to appear to be abreast of every on-dit. Juliet Lawley had not been present at the ball last night, which Ailsa had regretted. She had meant to put herself out to be highly agreeable to that young woman to lessen as far as she could the blow of her brother's capricious behavior.

Bridie, engaged in the outer room in putting a timely stitch to one of her mistress's day dresses, heard a shriek from the bedroom. She dropped the sewing and hurried in, to find that Lady Ailsa had spilled her chocolate and was endeavoring to get out of bed, still holding the sheets of the *Gazette*.

"Oh, no—never mind the chocolate, Bridie. Send to ask if Lord Spendale is awake. I want to see him— ask if he will step this way."

As Bridie sped on her errand, Lady Ailsa stared perplexedly at the news-sheet. It was not possible! Why had he said nothing to her? She read the notice again and again. It was clear enough. "The betrothal is announced...." Spendale and Juliet Lawley! Was ever a brother so provoking!

She glanced at the little Cloisonné clock beside her bed. Gone noon! Spendale must be up, unless he had come back last night badly in liquor. She thrust her feet into her slippers and hurriedly drawing her wrapper around her set off along the corridor to her brother's room. In the dressing room she found Bridie speaking to Jamie Leckie. Ailsa signed to Bridie to go back to her room and said quickly: "Where is Lord Spendale, Leckie? Has he gone riding?"

"No, your ladyship. His lordship did—did not return to the house last night," said Leckie delicately.

Lady Ailsa forebore to comment. It was not unknown for Spendale to spend nights away from the house, and one did not inquire what he did, for all her impertinent strictures upon his way of life. She merely said now that when he returned she wished to see him. Back in her room, Bridie was dealing with the spilt chocolate. Lady Bray, she said, was still asleep.

Ailsa did not wish to disturb her. There was little that Aunt Kirsty would say that could be of any help. Ailsa felt she must talk to someone. Gavin was with his regiment at Colchester. Neil was in Leicestershire. Tears pricked Ailsa's eyes as she struggled into a gown with Bridie's help. Neil... how must he feel? Ailsa could not bear that there should be any ill feeling between her brothers.

How could Spendale be so unfeeling as to absent himself on such a morning! Or had he celebrated his engagement by getting beastly drunk? And where was he? There would be visitors. All London would have read the announcement....

Lady Ailsa sat fuming while Bridie dressed her hair. She did not wish to remain in the house coping alone with a stream of congratulatory visitors talking about a matter of which she had as little knowledge as they themselves. There was no one in the Polite World she wished to see at that moment, and since she must talk to someone or burst, she naturally soon thought of Miss Fielding. Bridie was sent to tell a footman to get a chair for her mistress, and Lady Ailsa was soon on her way to Dane Street.

She found Miss Fielding walking in the garden behind the shop, looking so unwell that Lady Ailsa's first words were to apologize for disturbing her, but Eliane, after a first surprised gasp at the sight of Lord Spendale's sister, was sufficiently self-possessed to congratulate her on the forthcoming nuptials.

"Oh, you have seen it, too," said Lady Ailsa dismally.

It had in fact been Maria Taylor who had seen the *Gazette* that morning, and who had come running to Eliane to tell her. Maria had been as loyally silent about that meeting in the park as Miss Fielding had trusted she would be, and she had never commented, even to Ned, upon the strange coincidence that Eliane had been taken into Ardmore House after her street accident, but she naturally felt that Eliane would have some interest in the engagement of these members of high society.

Eliane had admitted to the interested Maria that she had also met Lord Spendale's betrothed while at Ardmore House, but showed little inclination to discuss the romance. Maria departed back to her duties in the shop with the feeling that Ned's half-sister was inexplicably dull at times. Lady Ailsa Ardmore was more perceptive but still did not relate Miss Fielding's obvious indisposition to the news of her brother's betrothal. She was convinced in her own mind that Miss Fielding would marry the eminently suitable Mr. Gretton, and was much occupied with her own distress at the possible estrangement of her brothers.

"Oh, Miss Fielding, I must confide my feelings to someone, and I count you my dearest friend, although I see you so seldom. How could Spendale have done this without a word? Truly one never knows what he will be at! And Juliet Lawley—can she have no feeling for Neil?"

Eliane forced herself to make some tactful comment, that Mr. Ardmore would doubtless find himself a wife who loved him truly, and that she wished Lord Spendale and Miss Lawley the greatest happiness.

The two girls stayed a while in the pleasant garden while Lady Ailsa poured out her feelings regarding her family problems, including her determination to marry Mr. Mackerras, but at last she said regretfully that she must return to see if Spendale had come back to Ardmore House. When she arrived in Park Lane, it was to find that Lady Bray was up and receiving visitors, one of whom had been Mrs. Ross. Lord Spendale had still not returned.

Mrs. Ross had professed herself highly gratified at the announcement but desired to know where Lord Spendale might be. That long suffering and conscientious chaperone had no wish to reveal to the world that Miss Lawley was missing, and now, although she was careful not to show surprise to Lady Bray, it seemed that both the lovers were out of town. Could they have gone together? She too left after a brief visit, to hurry back to Portman Square to see if a message had arrived from her missing charge. She found that a message had indeed arrived, but it was hardly reassuring or informative. Miss Lawley merely stated that she would be absent from Portman Square for a day or so and that explanations would be forthcoming later. Mrs. Ross was on no account to raise a hue and cry.... She could only think that perhaps since the young couple had flirted and bickered so much to the entertainment of polite society that they had fled the town after making their announcement. It was no way to go on, but one could only hope that all would be satisfactorily explained. In spite of her opinion of the frivolous nature of Lord Spendale's character, she had thought he had enough worldly shrewdness to avoid such a gaucherie as this unexplained flight, but Juliet she knew had odd ideas on romance.

The rest of the day passed with no appearance from his lordship. Lady Ailsa passed a restless night, and when Leckie informed her with a slightly more worried air that his master had still not returned, Ailsa sent hurriedly to Neil in Leicestershire. Something was wrong, she was sure of it now. If Spendale had taken his fiancée out of town, he would surely not have left his household without a word, nor fail to summon Leckie to join him.

In Leicestershire, as in the whole of the country, the weather turned suddenly for the worse. High winds blew from the east, and at sea ships ran for shelter or tried to ride it out some safer distance from the shore. Thomas Denby at Melbury Hall had been up early as was his custom, but since the weather was so bad, had spent some time in the gun room. His wife and brother-in-law were partaking of a leisurely breakfast together and waiting for him to join them for coffee when Neil Ardmore, who had been turning the pages of the London papers suddenly said abruptly:

"Forgive me, Meg," and brushed past the footman out of the room.

Startled, Lady Margaret had looked up from her perusal of the *Ladies Journal* to see that Neil had looked extremely disturbed. She heard him mutter "Morning, Tom," as Mr. Denby entered, and reached out to take the *Gazette* which her brother had been reading.

Thomas Denby settled himself at the table, and waited for his wife to pour his coffee. "What's the matter with Neil, Meg? Looked as if all the devils of hell were after him—well, now, you too! What now, Meg?"

"Tom, it's Spendale! He has announced his betrothal without a word to any of us—and it is to that American girl, Miss Lawley. Oh, Tom, this is worrying. She is the one Neil has wanted, I am sure of it!"

Thomas Denby grunted. "Well, they must sort it out between them. But I grant you it's a pity. Don't like embarrassments of that sort. Surely there are enough pretty girls that they don't have to fight over the same one?"

Lady Margaret poured the coffee, and then arose from the table, her agitation of mind not translated into her movements, which remained as calm and unhurried as ever. "I'll go and speak to him, Tom. He must be feeling badly."

Out in the hall, Neil was surprised to find one of the Ardmore servants there, badly travel-stained but bearing a letter from Lady Ailsa. The man had ridden post all the way from London to arrive on the same day as the *Gazette*, and now Neil Ardmore read his sister's frantic scrawl that she was amazed as he must be that Spendale had so announced his engagement to Miss Lawley, and what was queerer still was that he was missing. "He has neither left nor sent any message, nor taken any baggage with him, Leckie says. Oh Neil do you think he has come to some harm? Do you please return to London—Aunt Kirsty is no help at all," so the distracted Ailsa....

Neil looked up from the letter to find his twin standing beside him, her fair face troubled.

"Neil," she said gently. "I have read it in the *Gazette*. I am sorry."

Neil looked at her. His first impulse when he had read the *Gazette* was a desire to get his hands on his brother's throat. So this was why Spendale had got him out of London! But even in a short while, common sense reasserted itself. He knew his brother, and such hole-and-corner methods would run counter to his whole nature. If Spendale had wanted Juliet, he would not have got his brother out of London before he said so. Had they then come to an understanding, Juliet and Alastair? If so, he must bear it. But Neil had been sure that Spendale's interest lay elsewhere. In Miss Fielding, to be precise, though whether that would come to a marriage he had not been able to guess.

"Neil—" Margaret said again. "Don't take it so hard."

He held out Ailsa's letter to her. "This has arrived from Ailsa. She has sent it by Muir, who has ridden himself to a standstill. Spendale is missing. There is something odd here, Meg. I'm going back to town. My respects to your husband...."

She walked with him to his room, discussing the affair with him. It never took Neil long to arrange a journey. Within an hour he was on his way to Melton Mowbray, to continue to London by post chaise, taking Muir with him. A brief while at Ardmore House, where he heard more details from Ailsa, and he changed his traveling clothes for more suitable town wear, in order not to occasion comment, and then proceeded to Portman Square to obtain what information he might from Mrs. Ross.

He stayed with that lady long enough to extract everything she could remember, including a not-too-disguised account of Lord Spendale's behavior during his absence in Leicestershire, which caused a deep sigh to escape him. He thanked Mrs. Ross and promised to let her know the instant he knew anything definite of Miss Lawley's whereabouts.

Riding uneasily at anchor in the swift flow of the storm-roughened Thames, the *Savannah* had fared better than most ships. Some had lost their masts, while further upstream two laden barges had crashed against the piers of London Bridge and lost their cargoes. Aboard her father's ship, Juliet had grown weary of the constant buffeting and wished herself off the vessel, except that she had not been able to influence her prisoner. An excellent sailor himself, with apparently no nerves, he was in no way incommoded by the constant movement of the ship, and was blandly unaware, it seemed, of Miss Lawley's growing discomfort.

He continued to mend his broken head, and to reduce her to panic. She began to fear there was no easy way out of her dilemma. He passed the time amiably playing cards with the ship's officers, including the youthful Mr. Cramb, who now managed to combine his adoration of her beautiful self with a newly gained admiration, almost amounting to hero worship, of his fashionable lordship. Juliet suspected Spendale of deliberately setting himself to charm the boy on purpose to vex herself. She was bored with cards until she wished never to see another, but forced herself to join in.

After one such session, when the mate and the ship's surgeon had gone about their duties, Spendale glanced at her mutinous face. "You do not appear to find our company entrancing, Juliet?"

She turned on him in a sudden passion, so sick

was she of this tossing vessel, and all the trouble she had brought upon herself.

"I am so tired of this! You are only amusing yourself spinning it out. We could have been off the ship before this wretched storm, had you only seen reason!"

"Reason?"

"Oh, have done, my lord! I know that it pleases you now to keep me here, until *I* admit defeat! I might have known that I could not bend you to my will—"

"Well, then, your time has not been wasted. You have learned something."

"Lord Spendale—" she said desperately. "You do not know how matters stand. While you have been kept here, the notice of our betrothal has appeared in the *Gazette*—I sent it myself."

There—it was out now! She could only wait for a storm far worse to her than that which raged outside. After a silence in which all that could be heard was the howling wind and the incessant creaking of the ship's timbers, it came.

Spendale said incredulously: "You have *what*?"

She repeated what she had said, in a voice that shook. The change in him was daunting. For Spendale suddenly the jest was no longer a jest. His first thought was for Eliane. His second for Neil, who must think his brother had played him false. Gone was his pity for Juliet, his secret reproaches to himself, even his growing liking for her. He glared at her, and called her unhesitatingly a very unpleasant name, which made her flinch.

"I will not ask what you hoped to gain by such folly, Madam."

He threw the cards he had been shuffling down

upon the table. "You may put on your cloak, and give orders to your officers for a boat to be lowered. We are going ashore, immediately."

It was said so icily that she would not have known him for the same mocking companion.

"How *can* we go—in this weather? We shall have to wait for the storm to abate!"

"You heard me, Miss Lawley," he said evilly. "Do as you are bid."

She found, as had the Lady Ailsa before her, that when Spendale spoke in that tone, few would disobey him. She turned to leave the cabin. As the door opened, she fell back, buffeted by the wind. He came up behind her and assisted her to the upper deck, not so much out of courtesy as to make certain she continued to obey him. Above the wind, she shouted her request to Mr. Sully the mate, who was at that moment making his way across the upper deck.

They were immediately advised against any such project. The wind might drop by the next day. They would be well advised to delay their departure. His lordship's face remained set, his purpose inflexible.

Juliet stared out through the flying spume at the rough water. The recent heavy rains had swollen the volume of water coming downstream, and the tide was flowing swiftly toward the sea, against the strong easterly.

"No—no—" she said in sudden apprehension. The gray turbulent water menaced her. "It is madness. We cannot reach the shore!"

He merely said that she must expect the seamen to know their job. She saw in despair that he was in such a cold fury that he would not be halted, against all reason.

Spendale intended to reach the shore and make

speed to London. He could not doubt that the announcement in the *Gazette* had attracted attention, and Miss Fielding would almost certainly have heard of it. She should not remain under such a misapprehension for a moment longer than necessary. He had no pity for Juliet. She should return with him and face whatever embarrassments came from a public retraction.

A boat was lowered. With difficulty, Miss Lawley was assisted in, and the two brawny sailors pulled away. Huddled amidships, she would not look at Spendale. One glance had shown him completely unperturbed by the turbulence of the water. Eventually, as they appeared to make steady progress, she relaxed a little. It seemed that after all he was right. They would reach the shore.

Slowly they completed half the distance, passing other ships and barges tossing at anchor, when suddenly there was a great thud against the side of the boat, and anxious shouting. The barges which had been wrecked upstream by the bridge had spilled their cargoes of huge logs, and some of these were now hitting against the side of the boat, spinning it this way and that as they flowed out with the tide.

Suddenly the boat fouled yet another obstacle, and Juliet, paralyzed with terror, found that the river had come up to meet her. She screamed and sank beneath the water. Then she was above water again, as Spendale held her. The two sailors could only try to reach the logs.

Choking and gasping, she heard him shout: "Juliet! Lie still—still, I tell you. Trust me!"

She tried to obey, but the impulse to struggle was overwhelming. He shouted to her again: "Keep still—and you will be safe!" He shifted his grip to keep her higher. "I can reach another ship if you lie still—"

She managed to obey him, and after a few moments, as he fought his way through the water, she had the strange, heartbreaking pleasure of hearing him say: "Good girl—trust me—"

But in spite of his efforts, the tide carried him past the ship toward which he had been heading. He began to know with growing desperation that he was tiring. To cleave naked and untrammeled through the waters of Loch Garrick was one thing. To swim fully clothed in the Thames trying to support a girl whose full skirts dragged her down was another. The wound in his head throbbed badly. He kicked on doggedly, never needing his courage and his strength more than he did then. . . .

He turned his head, trying to glimpse the distant shore and gauge his progress. It seemed too far away for comfort.

But someone was shouting. He thought he could discern a boat with two men at the oars, and it was coming closer. It gave him new heart, and he fought on.

"Help is coming, Juliet," he said in her ear. The voices came nearer, shouting against the wind. She could hear the noise of the oars in the rowlocks, and forced herself to remain passive. Then incredibly she felt him laugh faintly and he said something in a foreign tongue which she could not understand. Another voice answered the time-honored greeting in Gaelic, and Neil Ardmore, bending swiftly, began to lift her into the other boat.

When he had called upon Mrs. Ross, Neil had gained enough information to give him cause to think. Juliet had undoubtedly been upset at her apparent failure to secure his brother, and if she had just then received the letters from home by way of one of her father's vessels, the Captain of which was personally known to her, it seemed a possibility that she had visited the ship. He thought, in agreement with Mrs. Ross, that Spendale and Juliet having at last come to an understanding and announced their betrothal, had decided to avoid the curious and stay a while aboard the vessel. He therefore went to Mr. Lawley's London agents and to Lloyds to learn of the ship, that it was indeed the *Savannah* as Mrs. Ross recalled, and was now lying off Deptford.

What did strike Neil as odd was that Spendale had left no message, and taken neither his man nor a change of clothing. A further disturbing thought had come when he visited some livery stables off Piccadilly and had met an acquaintance there who was inclined to express at length his views on the parlous state of the country in general, and the navy in particular. His Majesty's ships, he said, were so short of men that the pressgangs were getting bolder and less discriminating. He himself had seen a well dressed man taken near the Strand one night, but had not been near enough to interfere.

Neil could hardly suppose that the unfortunate individual had been his brother, but something strange had happened to Spendale, and he thought his first action should be to confirm whether or not he was aboard the *Savannah*.

At Deptford he had failed to find a boatman willing to take out his craft in such a storm, but as Neil's sharp eyes searched the gloom toward where the *Savannah* lay, her masts bare and tilting as she rode at anchor, he had seen the accident as the logs came downstream. Swiftly he offered the boatman fifty guineas if he should put out, and offered to take an oar himself that they should make better speed toward those bobbing heads.

Now as he and Spendale helped Juliet into the tossing boat, he moved quickly. His cape, only but a little drier than Juliet's sodden dress, was wrapped around her. He then took off his coat and passed it to Spendale, who at first shook his head. "Take it," said Neil. "I am taking an oar—we shall get back the quicker."

He unstoppered a flask of whisky and bending down, bade Juliet take a little. Once more she thankfully obeyed, and as the fiery liquid warmed her, she stole a glance at him. He had turned to give the flask to Spendale, and did not see that shy, desperate look. Never had Neil looked so calm, so dependable, so handsome nor so unutterably dear to her. She knew it now, as if the fast flowing murky waters of the Thames had taken with them all her foolishness. She watched him as he plied the oar with easy strength in time with the Thames waterman, and then closed her eyes in bitterness of remorse. She could not doubt she had lost him. The madness that had possessed her had made her offend beyond expectation of forgiveness.

At last the boat grounded, and she was helped out, up the rough slope of the river bank, an Ardmore brother on either side of her, toward an inn whose lights were showing with a promise of warmth and comfort.

The landlord and his wife hurried to do their best for them. The inn was crowded with delayed travelers sheltering from the weather, but a parlor was cleared for them and the fire built up to a blaze. As the servants hurried to put clean sheets on the beds upstairs, Juliet waited by the hearth with Spendale while Neil went to check upon their accommodation. His lordship was recovering his strength, but the bandage on his head was a sorry mess, and once again Juliet blamed herself.

She turned to him, and said almost inaudibly but with dignity: "I must thank you."

He looked down at her. That hard fight for survival in the Thames had had its effect upon him, too. "You have little enough to thank me for, Juliet," he said gently. "We have both been a pair of fools." He gave her such a smile as she would once have given much for. "I trust that one day we may be on much better terms. Believe me, I wish you all happiness."

Could he mean Neil? But Neil, who had come through the doorway but a moment before, to see them standing so close, whispering quietly, and to see her gaze up at his brother as he kissed her hand, was now staring into the glowing fire, his face unrevealing.

Soon she was put to bed amidst sheets that smelled of lavender, a hot brick wrapped cozily at her feet, her clothes taken away to be dried by the kitchen fire. In another room, Spendale proceeded to strip off and dry his lean body with a rough towel. He still intended to get to London without delay, and bade the landlord borrow some dry garments for him, and to get him a horse or a vehicle of some kind.

"Don't be a fool," said Neil shortly. "You need a rest, for some hours at least. A message may be sent later. Besides, there are some matters to be cleared up between us." He added curiously: "How did you get that head injury?"

"I understand that I fell down a companionway,

not being used to ships," said Spendale.

Neil knew him to be as surefooted as a lynx, and looked sharply at him, but merely said: "I will dress it for you."

The landlord brought strips of linen for bandages, and took away his lordship's clothes to dry. It took the good man some time to procure some breeches and a coat and his own best shirt which he said apologetically were not what the gentleman would wish. Spendale looked at the rough attire and saw that it was clean, and said indifferently that it would serve.

To Neil as the landlord went out of the room he said: "You are right. There must be explanations." And he proceeded to explain, shielding neither Juliet nor himself. Neil listened, and then said: "I should plant you a facer, to treat her so. She must have been desperate indeed, to do so crazy a thing. It's a damnable coil, but I do not want her humiliated. Can you delay the correction a few days? As long as the family know you are safe, perhaps you will lie low for a week? I had thought I might take her to Leicestershire. If she stays out of town for a while until the matter dies down, it will be easier for her."

Spendale nodded in agreement. He held out the bandages for his brother to attend to his injured head. "You may plant me that facer some other time. The moment is hardly suitable." He smiled wryly. "There is in my writing desk at home a half finished letter to you that might make you think less badly of me. She has suffered nothing from me but humiliation to her vanity, and I think that is past. I have been hard with her, but I had no thought to drive her to such an indiscretion. My intentions were for your happiness. Perhaps it is remorse, but I have come to like her a good deal more. You were right, I am sure."

"Right?" Neil sent him a sharp glance.

"Yes. That there is another Juliet."

Neil was silent, and then said: "I suggest you send a note to Mrs. Ross to inform her that Juliet is at Meg's. It will sound the most reasonable thing in the circumstances, and then a further announcement to the *Gazette* may be sent from Leicestershire in a few days' time."

"As you wish. But there is one other person who must be told that the announcement is a mistake."

"Miss Fielding?" Once more Neil Ardmore looked keenly at his brother. "Do you think to marry her, Spendale? I know that the decision must be yours alone, but I take it that there are difficulties."

"You may take it so. And the decision is not mine. So far she will not have me," he answered with some bitterness. "But at least I must attempt to see her. She must have read that damned lie in the *Gazette*."

They continued to talk a while, but in spite of his obvious fatigue, Spendale insisted on returning to town that evening. Ailsa and Aunt Kirsty must have their minds put at rest, he said. Neil saw him off on a returning post-horse, the postboy riding in company. Spendale promised to send Neil's man with some of Miss Lawley's wardrobe, to be obtained from Portman Square.

The next morning, Neil sent to Miss Lawley to ask if she would join him for breakfast, should she feel well enough to do so. She came hesitantly into the back parlor, attired still in her dried but ruined clothes. The red-gold curls were soft and disordered from her immersion. Neil sprang to his feet and greeted her with formal kindness, but as her first words were to ask timidly if Lord Spendale had gone, the atmosphere of constraint was not lessened.

With some degree of stiffness, he put forward his suggestion that she should accompany him to his sister's house in Leicestershire, and from there take her time over future decisions.

"To Lady Margaret's?" Juliet flushed with shame and pleasure combined. "Oh, I should like that." She looked up at him gratefully, and bit her lip to still its sudden quivering.

"You are being very kind," she said.

He only said formally: "Not at all. We must all wish the matter settled as easily as possible."

Once she might then have challenged him, asked if he did not consider that she had disgraced herself? Now she could not. To do so would imply that she felt she had a battle to fight, and there was no fight left in her, only a quiet dignity which made her accept his help with gratitude, but ask no more of him. After the arrival of his manservant and her own maid with a box of her clothes from Portman Square, together with a rather baffled message from Mrs. Ross, they set out in a post chaise for Lady Margaret Denby at Melbury Hall.

As it was a fine morning, although the wind was still strong, Neil chose to ride outside. When they stopped for a change of horses, he obtained refreshment for her, but confined his conversation to politeness. She knew he had a habit of silence, but it had once been a curiously companionable silence between them. Now she was eager for any word, even of recrimination, for that might at least hint that he still had some feeling for her. As the miles sped by, on a journey which once might have given her the greatest pleasure, she knew that although she might count upon a courteous reception from his twin sister, it could reflect no more than the same kindness that he was showing. Juliet felt sure that to the Ardmore family she must appear a vulgar and vexatious acquaintance whom they would be glad to drop as soon as they conveniently could.

Neil continued to ride beside the chaise. His thoughts were his own.

They stopped at Melton Mowbray for their last change of horses before proceeding to Melbury Hall. Juliet could bear it no longer. As Neil came into the inn parlor to tell her that the chaise was once more ready, she said hesitantly:

"Forgive me—you have not said what you will tell your sister of this hateful business—"

He looked surprised. "Why, only that you and my brother have regretted your impulse, and now wish to withdraw from your engagement with as little publicity as possible."

"But for me to come to Leicestershire—will she not think it strange?"

"Not at all. She knows that you are a visitor to this country—that your own home is in America." He smiled faintly. "When you know Meg, you will see that it is nothing unusual for the family to bring their difficulties to her. But she need know nothing of the truth of the matter. Pray be easy, Miss Lawley."

Riding once more inside the chaise, Juliet did not observe that Mr. Ardmore's manservant was no longer in the party, but was in fact riding ahead to Melbury Hall with a message from his master. Juliet found herself welcomed by a tall and stately young woman, whose likeness to Neil Ardmore made her catch her breath a little, and whose natural kindliness of disposition was obvious and comforting. It seemed that Miss Lawley's appearance in Leicestershire while the engagement was publicly broken was the most natural thing in the world. She was welcomed, and taken to her room to rest from her journey.

Nevertheless, Lady Margaret hurriedly sought her brother.

"And now, Neil, an explanation, if you will! Your note was necessarily brief, but why have *you* brought her here, and not Spendale? There is a mystery here! What has gone wrong?"

"Only that Miss Lawley and Spendale wish to withdraw from their hasty betrothal. Obviously it will cause chatter which they wish not to face. Spendale is making his own arrangements. I have brought Juliet to you, until she decides what further to do."

Lady Margaret threw up her hands. "As I live, I shall never understand Spendale!" She regarded her other brother with affection, "But you, Neil, does it mean that Miss Lawley has come to realize that it is you she wants?"

He smiled wryly. "We cannot jump to such a conclusion. Pray ask her no questions, Meg. She has undergone a good deal of emotional upset, and needs kindness and privacy."

"She shall have both," said Margaret Denby warmly. "Pray trust me to warn Tom to be discreet."

Neil had no fear of his brother-in-law. He and Meg were a well-matched pair. As he went to his own room, he wondered a little how Spendale was managing his affairs in London. He wished him well.

* * *

Lord Spendale had reached London late that night, and gone straight to Ardmore House. The servants gaped as his lordship strode in attired in such garments as they had never thought to see him in, but there was no change in his manner. He merely requested that Leckie should attend him at once, and in spite of his fatigue was running upstairs to his room when Lady Ailsa, having heard his voice, came swiftly from the drawing room.

"Spendale—oh, thank God! Where can you have been?"

She took further stock of him after he had released himself from her encircling arms. "What has happened? Why are you wearing such clothes? You look like a footpad!"

"My thanks," he said sarcastically. "Ailsa, pray tell our aunt that I am returned, but no details, if you please. Then come to my room."

She did as she was bidden and agog with curiosity lost no time in returning to his room, to find him in a silk dressing gown and Leckie and the housemaids bringing water for a hot bath. He dismissed them and then said: "Ailsa, you will have to wait for explanations. Meanwhile, I have some unfinished business with Miss Fielding. But I cannot call at her home. I don't as yet wish the town to know that I have returned. Can you arrange a meeting for me?"

Ailsa stared. "Miss Fielding!" He was more and more mysterious! What could Miss Fielding have to do with what concerned them most—his marriage to Juliet Lawley? "You want to see Eliane?" she repeated. She had ceased to think that her brother might have any real interest in Miss Fielding after his initial error had been apologized for. She had thought that he preferred to forget the whole embarrassing episode, and had come to think of Eliane solely as her own particular friend and confidante.

"I have said so," he said impatiently.

"Well, I do know that she is going to the masked ball at the Opera House tomorrow night. In company with Mr. Gretton."

"Then send for a mask and domino for me—for us both, if you were not going," he said swiftly. He stared at his sister suddenly as a new notion came to him. "You have seen her lately, Ailsa? Does she know of the announcement in the *Gazette*?"

"All London knows of it," said his sister tartly.

"And how did you find Miss Fielding—was she well and in spirits?"

"Indeed she was not," said Lady Ailsa with uncommon obtuseness. "I thought she looked positively unwell, but she is determined to go to the charity ball at the Opera House."

"Then we shall also contribute to a good cause," he said with a sudden smile. "Now I'm going to have a bath and some sleep. Remember to tell Aunt Kirsty nothing but that I have returned and all is well."

He was already feeling a good deal better. As Jamie Leckie dealt skillfully with his head wound, Spendale's spirits rose. Not unversed in the ways of the female heart, it occurred to him, if not to Lady Ailsa, that Miss Fielding's indisposition might be caused by the announcement of his forthcoming marriage to Miss Lawley. Perhaps Juliet had unwittingly done him a good turn....

His sudden good humor was in such marked contrast to his mood of late that Leckie, who was no older than his master, smiled a little as he drew the curtains around his lordship's bed. Spendale thought a while of Eliane, and then fell into a dreamless sleep.

CHAPTER EIGHT

THE masked ball at the Opera House was for a favorite charity for destitute children, and the brilliant crowd contained many of the nobility who had paid generously for their tickets. Some complained that the crush was frightful. The floor was half the time too crowded for the set dances, and as for the promenade, as Lady Herrick said, if you lost someone in the crowd you were not likely to see them again.

Lord Spendale stood in the shadows seeking for Eliane. London seemed that night to be populated by slender females five and a half feet tall. The all enveloping dominoes made his task all the harder.

It was easier for Eliane. His height made him stand out above the men, and she had developed a habit of searching out for tall figures in any public gathering she attended. As she turned this way and that in a cotillion, she glanced continually to see that he remained where he was, masked and in an unobtrusive dark green domino, always scanning the crowds. It seemed as if he had not come to greet his friends nor to take part in the merry making. At last, contrary to her intention, he became aware of the glances of the lady in the forget-me-not blue domino and wondered, once he had checked that her partner was probably Lionel Gretton, that he could have taken so long to see her.

He now kept her under close observation, noting those she spoke to and following her with her party to the box they had taken. He waited impatiently for an opportunity to speak to her alone, and when her companions left to dance once more, leaving her alone in the box with Gretton, Spendale swiftly beckoned to one of the Opera House servants, and gave him a coin to inform the gentleman in a certain box, if he should answer to the name of Mr. Gretton, that a gentleman desired to speak urgently with him in the foyer. He shortly had the satisfaction of seeing Mr. Gretton hurry away, and went at once to the box where Miss Fielding sat alone, leaning forward to watch the dancers, and in fact wondering where the tall figure had gone.

She gave a gasp as the green domino came into the box, shutting the door behind him. She rose to her feet at once, and fluttering her fan vivaciously, informed the intruder in voluble French that M'sieu had mistaken the box.

Spendale ignored her tactics. "Eliane, I must speak to you—I have got rid of Gretton for a few minutes."

She instantly gave up her pretense of not knowing him. "Good evening to you, Lord Spendale. Mr. Gretton will not be pleased. And I must felicitate you and Miss Lawley on your betrothal. I wish you very happy."

"Do you?" he said hardly. He came closer. "You

never believed that wretched announcement!"

"Why not? I understand that such a happy outcome has long been foreseen—"

"Oh, have done! Will you believe it when I tell you that it is all a rig? I cannot explain now, but it was never so. Surely you *must* believe me!"

As she did not answer, he said vexedly: "Eliane, pray take off that infernal mask. I cannot see your face." He removed it himself before she could stop him. "Will you listen to me, in a day or so, once I have disentangled myself from this business?"

"You are under no obligation to make any explanations to me, my lord." But she looked up apprehensively as he came closer.

"I have proposed marriage to you twice, my girl—three times if you will count this also, and I have kissed you only once, and that before I loved you—" As he went to take hold of her, intense longing swept through Eliane in such a way as she had never known. She wanted to touch him, to fold her arms around him, to kiss his face.... Insensibly she too moved, almost into his arms, and then hastily drew back.

For a moment he had thought he had won at last, but her recoil was only too obvious.

"Dear God—can I not warm you into *some* feeling for me?" he said in desperate humiliation.

Her fan fluttered agitatedly as she drew away. "Please, my lord, I see Mr. Gretton returning—"

"Gretton!" he said angrily. "What is he to you?"

"Something," said Eliane valiantly, "that you are not, Lord Spendale."

She felt safe in the ambiguity of her words, and turned with apparent eagerness to the approaching Mr. Gretton. It was too much for Spendale. "Oh, damnation," he said under his breath. "I have had enough. You may marry whom you will, you jade!"

Mr. Lionel Gretton eyed his visitor with no love. "It is you, my lord, whom I have to thank for a fool's errand?" he said belligerently.

"My apologies, Mr. Gretton," said the Viscount Spendale with insulting indifference. "But also my congratulations on being able to persuade the lady to make up her mind. I wish you both happy!"

He did not look at her again, but bowed and left them.

Lionel Gretton turned with sudden hope. "What did he mean, Miss Fielding? Am I to understand—?"

"Oh, no. Please! This is abominable. He was but funning, Mr. Gretton."

He heard the sob in her voice.

"Confound his impudence! Nothing would give me greater pleasure than to call him out for annoying you—"

"Oh, no, no, please, Mr. Gretton," she laid a restraining hand upon his arm. "Do not blame him— he is sorely tried."

Lionel Gretton gave her an odd look, and then said in his more usual measured tones: "I think we might take supper now, Miss Fielding, if the crush has lessened?"

She tried hard to be gay company for the rest of the evening, not wishing to spoil his enjoyment or arouse the curiosity of their companions. She forced herself to stay nearly to the end, aware that the tall figure in the green domino had gone. Mr. Gretton brought her home in his carriage to Dane Street, to be let in by Molly, who shot the bolts behind her, and said that the rest of the household had retired.

Eliane climbed the stairs slowly toward her room. On the first floor, the sitting room door was ajar, and she could see the glowing embers of the fire in the darkness. She went in for a moment, and stood looking down at the quietly smoldering logs. The tears rolled down her face. To feel his vexation with her ... to be called a jade!

Mr. Fielding, who had sat there late with his own thoughts, and had not troubled to light a fresh candle, now said softly: "Eliane?" as he heard a telltale sniff.

"Oh, Papa! I had no notion you were there! Sitting in the dark! You were not waiting up for me? Mr. Gretton brought me home safely—"

"Did you enjoy yourself, child?"

"It was very crowded," she said. She hoped he had not seen the tears, but Mr. Fielding rose from his chair and brought a candle from the side table and lit it from the fire. He set it upon the mantelshelf and turned to regard her thoughtfully.

"Let us talk a little, Eliane, while everyone is abed." He paused, and then said gently: "What are we to do with you, child? You will not have Mr. Gretton, and weeks ago you refused Lord Spendale—"

"You know it would never serve, Papa. His circumstances are so far beyond!"

Mr. Fielding sighed. "I have been a selfish parent, Eliane. When I married your stepmother I thought I had taken the right decision for your welfare—"

"So did you," she said eagerly. "We have all been content—most happy, Papa!"

"Just so—until my Eliane grows up. I have known for some time that you are not happy now, my dear.

If you had seen fit to accept Mr. Gretton I should have been pleased, but it was not to be. And Lord Spendale has now chosen elsewhere, it seems." He was silent for a moment and then resumed: "I must tell you that after much thought—and I will admit, reluctance—I have written to your grandfather to ask if he will acknowledge you."

"Papa!" For a moment she could not speak, so utterly unexpected was his statement. "But why?"

"Surely you see that if your mother's family accept you, you will enter the world upon different terms than you do now? How else will you find a husband such as you deserve? You are right to say that Mrs. Fielding has made us all happy, but the inheritance of your blood demands more. I have realized it for some time."

Her father's action was to her so astounding and so unlike what she had ever believed him capable of, that she still could not speak for a while. Then at last, the words poured from her agonizedly, like the breaking of a dam, reproaching him at last as she had never believed that she would.

"Oh, Papa! How could you? How I wish you had not! I am English—not French! I am *your* daughter. Eliane Fielding!" She stressed the English name, but gave a little sob. She believed she was not even entitled to that! Her dark blue eyes were stormy. "How could they acknowledge me?" she said passionately. "What standing should I have in their great family? I will not go to be despised and slighted!" Overwrought with the emotions that had torn her in her painful passage with Lord Spendale, she burst into tears. "Oh, Papa, dearest Papa, why ever would they not permit you to marry Mamma? How could they have been so cruel, so cruel!"

There was an astounded silence in the room as Mr. Fielding gazed in blank amazement at his daughter. He thought for a moment that his sensible child had lost her wits.

"*What* are you saying, Eliane?" he said at last.

She choked with her sobs. "I do not blame you, dearest Papa. Nor Mamma. I honor her memory. I would not have spoken—I thought never to let you know that I knew! It was her family—her hateful family—her father. They prevented you marrying her. I have known of it ever since I was a child! Naturally I could never ask you—a grief to you—The French servants that we had, Babette and Marie-Simone! I heard them talking—I have always known, you see!"

Charles Fielding was appalled. "My poor child, I do not know what you thought you heard! How old were you? Eight, nine? Either they lied, gossiping ignorantly, or you misunderstood what they were saying, in your childish innocence. Of course I married your mother! There is no question! What rights would I have had over you otherwise? Her father and brother took her back by force and you were born in the Château de Varency. She died, and it was years before I could compel them to give you up, by dint of threats of exposure and suits at law! I have detested them, but you, my poor Eliane, how you must have suffered from this terrible misapprehension! It is my fault—" he said with an agitation which matched her own. "From never wishing to parade my grief, I have spoken of your mother as seldom as possible. I little knew the harm I have done you!"

Eliane felt an enormous burden lifted from her, and her only thought now was to comfort her father lest he reproach himself too much for a mistake that had been hers alone. "You must not blame yourself, Papa. You could not have known the mistake I made. Dearest and best Papa, I know you have always loved me. But I do not wish ever—ever to have anything to do with Mamma's family. I could only loathe them as you do. They are vile!"

Mr. Fielding shook his head. "They loved her, too. It was their family pride. You must appreciate how it is in France. The French nobility are so remote from the people. To them, a mere English tutor, I was less than dust! She had disgraced herself in their eyes beyond anything they could comprehend! In England it is different. There is rank, and much attention paid to it, but there is often respect and it is not impossible for the classes to mingle." He broke off. "I have acted as I thought best, Eliane. There is no reason why the Marquis de Varency should not acknowledge you. You are his legitimate granddaughter, even though but the daughter of an impoverished English scholar of no lineage! But if you wish, no more need come of it!"

She felt reassured, and kissed him affectionately. She said they should think no more of it. If she never married at all, she was content to stay his daughter.

Thus said Miss Fielding, but Charles Fielding was not so old that he could not remember his passionate love for her mother. He smiled wryly, chucked her under the chin, and said the matter could rest.

In her room, the daughter of Eliane de Varency stood in her night shift by her window, looking out over the trees in the garden. It was too late now. Believing herself not legally entitled even to the name of Fielding, she had preferred persistently to reject Alastair Ardmore rather than have him enter a marriage he would come to regret.

"Oh, my love, my love," breathed Miss Fielding.

Had he truly not proposed to Miss Lawley? How could that be? He was unpredictable and contrary, with a swift temper and an arrogant cast of mind, but she knew that had matters gone differently, she might have dealt with him very well. He had said he needed her. She knew he did. But it was too late.

CHAPTER NINE

In Leicestershire Miss Lawley found something she had never expected, a haven of peace where her bruised spirit might mend. She had traveled to Melbury Hall expecting no more than a convenient if somewhat embarrassing bolt-hole from whence she might make her arrangements to travel across England to Bristol and then to take ship to America, leaving her heartache behind her. Now as the days passed in slow undemanding tranquillity, she knew it would be a wrench to leave.

Melbury Hall was unlike anything else she had yet seen in England. Bristol had been pleasing and exciting, a great seaport where the splendid houses of wealthy merchants were a foretaste of the grandeurs of London. London had indeed proved splendid—splendid and squalid, a city of hectic gaiety for a Colonial heiress. There she had found a bewildering variety of people, whose skillful insincerities and flatteries had set her values awry until she headed for disaster. Now the long low-built Tudor manor house with its creeper-covered mullioned windows, smooth-shaved lawns and splendid trees and gardens showed her another England, quieter and timeless. The gardens were a particular delight to her, and such time as she did not spend in the nursery marveling at the beauty of Master James Philip Neil Gifford Denby was spent in walking about the gardens of the Hall.

Lady Margaret was friendly, shrewd and sometimes elusive. Neil Ardmore was also elusive. He seemed to spend a good deal of time out of doors, but not walking through yew alleys and rose terraces. It would appear that he shared his brother-in-law's interest in improving the quality of agriculture and that this absorbed their time. Miss Lawley was in fact left very much to her own devices and her own thoughts.

Evenings proved another matter, but were filled pleasantly enough with music and cards and sewing, with occasional visits from neighbors who never seemed to have read the *London Gazette*.

She was beginning to be able to speak to Neil with some semblance of ease. He would draw her out, getting her to talk of her home and family until she felt a whole person again, and not a mere social miscreant. Nevertheless her pensive face and the tears which on one occasion she had been surprised into revealing only confirmed to Neil Ardmore his belief that she still fretted for his brother.

Mr. Thomas Denby noticed nothing except that she was a pleasant young woman, good to look upon and a companion for his wife. Lady Margaret said little, asked a few questions, but thought a good deal. Her long-lashed blue eyes frequently flickered an unobtrusive glance at Miss Lawley's face when Neil was present, and her conclusions were not the same as her brother's. One day when Miss Lawley was occupied in the nursery and Neil Ardmore had not accompanied Mr. Denby, Meg called him into her dressing room.

"I am writing to Ailsa, Neil. Have you any messages?"

"Tell her to behave herself and not to lose too much at cards."

"And Spendale?"

Neil met her glance. "Only greetings."

"Neil—we have heard nothing from London since your arrival. Did you quarrel?"

"Of course not."

Meg sighed. "I see you will not tell me." Nevertheless, she thought that it would not be long before he and Miss Lawley resolved their affairs. Her mind was unaccustomedly upon her elder brother. "I wish," she said artlessly, "that Spendale would settle. Has the London season produced no suitable girl to keep him in order and make him happy?"

"I see that *you* will persist until you have got your answer."

"Well, Neil, there *is* something you do not tell me. Spendale is contrary enough, but he would not be so in the matter of choosing a wife! It is not like him to announce his betrothal and then change his mind. Does he still care for Miss Lawley?"

"I see you will have it, Meg. The truth is that he never cared for her. The whole thing was a stupid error—a bêtise—" He stopped abruptly, and then went on: "I confess it took me by surprise, but it is now undone. She will go back to America. I am not wholly in Spendale's confidence, but I may tell you I believe his affections to be engaged elsewhere."

"Well—now—" Meg looked pleased. "At last. Who is she?"

"I have met her," said Neil cautiously. "I can tell you no more, except that so far she will not have him. He is hopeful, I believe."

"Indeed?" Meg raised her brows. "This must be a healthy experience for Spendale!"

"I think he has found it painful."

"How glad I am that there were no difficulties with Tom and myself! But Neil, if you will not as yet say who she is, tell me at least—will she make him happy? Spendale needs to be happy!"

Neil raised his brows at her. "Don't we all?" he said with feeling.

"Spendale particularly." She glanced at her brother in sudden anxiety. "Neil! He has not involved himself with someone unsuitable? No, he cannot! For all his faults, he would not do that!"

"Although I know her so little, I do believe that if he secures her affections, he will be a fortunate man."

"Good, that is splendid. I cannot wait to call her sister, whoever she may be!"

Neil looked at her thoughtful face. "So much concern for Spendale, Meg! And why should he need, above all people, to be happy?"

She hesitated, and then went to the window, gazing out on to the terrace. "Neil, there is something I learned years ago, which I have never told even you. Do you remember when the south wing at Glengarrick was burned?"

"I remember—" he looked puzzled. "Our parents were away in Edinburgh. We were fourteen that day—it was our birthday, and a mighty fine time we had to save some furniture. There was a bureau I remember our father inquiring after most particularly, but it was burned beyond repair!"

"It did not survive our efforts to throw it from a window!" Meg smiled faintly, but was instantly serious. "Neil, there was a secret drawer in that desk. I found a letter—it was half-charred—I could not return it to Papa for then he would know someone had seen it." Her agitation grew. "He must have forgotten he had not destroyed it—he loves Mamma so much! Neil, it was from one of the servants to Papa. Did you ever know that Mamma and Papa were once seriously estranged? She ran away from him before Spendale was born! The letter was to tell Papa that he had a son—he did not know! And the letter said that Mamma had refused to set eyes on the child, had rejected him and sent him out to nurse, concealing his birth from Papa. Can you imagine it of Mamma? It seems that for almost two years Spendale was not known to be Glengarrick's son!"

Neil was frowning. "It were better if this had never come to light, Meg. I had heard once that our parents' early life was stormy, but this I had never suspected. If you have the letter still—no, you are too sensible not to have destroyed it!"

She shook her head. "I have it still. I was a little afraid. It was not clear to me whether Spendale was truly Papa's heir, or whether *you* were his eldest legitimate son. I did not know the cause of our parents' quarrel! But now I am sure that Spendale is truly Glengarrick's heir, and that Mamma did not—did not—"

Neil smiled reassuringly. "Our mother's honor is not in question! Spendale resembles her, but there is enough Ardmore in him to shout his paternity! Meg, my dear, our parents' past is their affair. Whatever their difficulties, they have lived in the greatest devotion anyone may hope to see, ever since I can remember. They were reconciled before our birth! So if you have the letter, burn it, and forget it."

Lady Margaret went to her own bureau and unlocked it, and unlocked yet again a small drawer within a drawer. She took out a heavily sealed package and handed it to her brother.

"Is this it?"

She nodded. He took it, and without breaking the seal, cast it into the flames of the log fire.

"I would not have Spendale troubled by the knowledge of such old griefs," he said.

Margaret watched the letter flare into ash, with a feeling of relief. "I have sometimes wondered if he *has* known of it," she said. "He has always been a little apart, hard—and somehow mocking—so often willfully refusing to take anything seriously! Perhaps it has influenced his character! And have you not seen how Mamma has a special feeling for him? So anxious to protect him when we were young, and to excuse all his faults, as if she blamed herself for his difficult temperament?"

"I do not deny that she has always sought to defend his flights," admitted Neil. "But what blame could attach to our mother? Spendale is Spendale. And if his better qualities do not always emerge—well, he may yet alter!"

"I have believed that Mamma blames herself—that her unhappiness before his birth must have affected him," said Meg.

"Fanciful female nonsense, Meg! As for her refusing to see him during his infancy—this was perhaps her loss, not his! How many men and women in the past have been put out to nurse from birth? Has it not been the custom? By your reckoning, they should all be marked for life! Don't be foolish Meg. Motherhood has made you fanciful and nervous!"

She smiled at him. Motherhood had indeed stirred her from her placidity. She knew that as she gazed at the rosy beauty of her infant son, she knew herself blessed as her own mother had not been in the birth of her first child. And she and Neil—did they not owe their more tranquil temperament to their mother's greater happiness when they were born? But she merely said: "We must wish Spendale happy. He has vexed Papa often enough, but he might settle—with the right wife!"

Neil said lightly: "He has settled more than you know. Being responsible for Ailsa has aged him, I swear it!"

She laughed. "You may be right! I will bid her be careful not to try him too hard."

They walked downstairs together and out into the rose garden. Neil's attention was caught by the sight of Miss Lawley down by the ornamental bridge over the lake, and he repressed a sigh, which was not lost upon his sister. Men, thought the Lady Margaret, with a sensation of discovery, were the oddest creatures.

The next day's post brought a two-day old *London Gazette* which contained a tactfully worded announcement that the marriage arranged between the Viscount Spendale and Miss Juliet Lawley would not now take place. Neil took it to Juliet and said gently: "There now, Miss Lawley, you may see that your difficulties are resolved."

She read the wording, while a flush stole over her

face. Perhaps one day she would be able to smile at this episode, but not yet!

"I have written to Mrs. Ross, asking her to stay with me in Bath, until a suitable vessel sails from Bristol," she said.

"You judge it best to go home to Virginia? England will not hold you now?"

"No—I wish to go home—it is where I belong."

If only he had said "Scotland" instead of England, she might have thought she had a hope, but it seemed as if he had no thought to renew his courtship. Lady Margaret received news of her intention with a startled glance at Neil. If ever two lovers seemed more willfully determined to part! Patiently she waited a further two days, but when arrangements were being made for Miss Lawley's journey to Bath, she felt it time to intervene.

"I shall be sorry to lose Miss Lawley," she remarked when once more alone with her brother. "I could have wished her stay much longer. I have come to like her very well."

"Yes, Meg," said Neil patiently.

"I could throw up my hands in despair! Are you not going to ask her hand?"

"To what end? You are a romantic matchmaker, Meg, but I am neither noble enough nor fool enough to bind myself to a wife who yearns for another man. I have a fancy to be wanted for myself!"

"Oh, Neil!" She was touched. "You deserve the greatest happiness. But I thought that you and Miss Lawley—"

"Surely you can see how matters stand?" he said savagely. "She is breaking her heart for Spendale!"

Margaret stared, while he glared back at her, and then she broke into an affectionate crow of laughter.

"Oh, Neil, you were never used to be such a slowtop! Indeed, she is breaking her heart, but it is not for *Spendale*!"

There was a moment's silence. Then he said uncertainly: "Meg—are you sure? You would not fool on such a matter? Have I been mistaken?" He looked at her with quick dawning hope. "Where is she?"

"Supervising her packing, I shouldn't wonder," said Margaret with a smile. "But I think I will send her for my sewing which I left in the summer house."

Miss Lawley was not sorry to leave her packing and to go in search of her ladyship's embroidery, but as she approached the summer house through the rose garden, she met Mr. Ardmore with the tambour frame in his hand.

"Oh! Mr. Ardmore—Lady Margaret asked me to find her sewing—"

Neil hung the tambour frame upon a rose bush. "I know. The merest device to give me a chance to speak to you in private. Juliet—tell me in all candor—do you still care for Spendale?"

For a moment she was silent, while her face went pink. Neil said hopelessly: "I see you do. My sister was mistaken—"

"No—oh, no!" gasped Juliet. "Please—you took me by surprise. And I do still suffer embarrassment—more than that—shame to remember my folly—" Her eyes pleaded with him.

Neil's face was strained. "But is it ended? I had not thought to ask you again. My love for you has never altered, but I have no mind to be a second best—"

"Second best?" breathed Juliet. "*Second* best? *You*? Oh, Neil!" Her eyes filled with tears.

He drew her to him, her copper head tilted in the

crook of his arm as he smiled down at her. "Dearest and best of men," she whispered. "Oh, Neil, forgive me—"

He kissed her then. Such a kiss as she had dreamed of, responding to him with such a hungry, desperate passion that he murmured: "Foolish girl—why did you not give me but a hint?"

"I?" she said. "How could I, after such folly! This time I had to wait, and it seemed to me that you must despise me. Neil, will it always lie between us, just a little?"

He shook his head. "It was a sickness, best forgotten. You are my Juliet again."

She yielded happily once more. They were in a world of their own. In the house, Lady Margaret thought her embroidery frame was a suitably long time in being returned, and she went upstairs to resume her letter to Lady Ailsa. From her window she could just see the summer house, and smiled.

CHAPTER TEN

In London, Dane Street continued its busy but mundane activities. Maria Taylor having discovered a second interesting announcement in the *Gazette* hastened to acquaint Miss Fielding with it, and was gratified to find that this time Ned's sister showed a greater interest. She even took hold of the newssheets and read it herself, although she was not to be prevailed upon to guess at what might have caused the breakdown of this particular romance.

Miss Fielding had in fact become noticeably unlike her usual self. The belief that she had been born out of wedlock had had its secret effect upon the molding of her character. It had made her impose upon herself standards unusually high, and had contributed to the astringent reserve in her manner. This in itself had increased the shock it had been to her when Alastair Ardmore had first behaved so regrettably at Vauxhall. There had even been moments when she wondered wildly if her bastardy had left some mark, that he could mistake her so. Now that she knew no such stigma clouded her life, she tried to be the same deliberately cool girl. But she could not. Her moods increased. Gaiety increased, only to alternate with moments of forlorn despair when she remembered that he had said he had had enough of her, and called her a jade.

No reply came from France, nor did she wish it.

They kept early hours in Dane Street because of the shop. Eliane occupied herself with sewing and embroidery, liking to make the delicate ruffles and ruchings which trimmed her dresses or edged her father's shirts, but it made a long day, and she too retired early, to be awakened one night by Molly, who came upstairs to whisper, with eyes like saucers, that the Lady Ailsa Ardmore was below, and asking if she might come up to Miss Fielding's room.

"Pray show her ladyship up, Molly—but quietly, mind." Eliane hid her astonishment at this late call, and flinging back the bedclothes, got up at once and put on a wrapper. Whatever the reason for this midnight visit, it must be something secret or urgent, or both. Life never proceeded very smoothly with Lady Ailsa to influence it.

She had evidently been to a party or the play. She looked extremely pretty but rather flushed. Her fashionably wideswept curls were powdered and pomaded, and threaded with a jeweled ribbon. Her gown of gossamer pink silk had flowers in silver thread work. Her fur trimmed cloak and hood of amethyst velvet hung loose around her as she came in.

"Eliane, pray get back into bed!" she commanded. "The evening has turned cold. May we have another candle?"

Eliane obediently sent for further candles, but sat

on the edge of her bed, awaiting Lady Ailsa's explanations. When Molly had returned with the candles and departed again, Ailsa began to speak in a rapid whisper. "Forgive me, Eliane. I had to come at this late hour. I am supposed to be at Lady Mayo's and must return soon before my absence is noticed."

She clutched Eliane's wrist firmly. "I need your help, Eliane. Gavin's regiment is sailing for India within days. They are quartered now near Dover. I must get to him and you must help me, oh, promise you will?"

"I?" said Eliane faintly.

"Yes—you are my only friend, the only one I can truly trust. I *need* you, Eliane. I need your support. I must marry Gavin before he sails and before Papa returns." She paused a moment. "I am desperate. Spendale has announced that we are to return to Glengarrick! He says he is sickened of London—did you ever hear such nonsense?—and will not leave me here by myself. I do not wish to go, but he is adamant. You have no idea what a pig he can be—how immovable against all reason! I asked him to let me go to Leicestershire, to my sister Meg's. After all, that is a good deal nearer Dover, although of course I did not stress that to *him*, but he said no. Neil and Juliet are there, and shortly to be married!"

"*What?*" Miss Fielding's tone was fainter still.

"Oh, yes, is it not astounding? I still do not know what happened with regard to Spendale. He will not say a word. I suppose we must consider it good news. It seems that Spendale does! He actually laughed, in the oddest way, and said to thank God something had gone well! Can he deliberately have sought to make her sick of himself, in order to throw her at Neil? There is never any knowing!"

Eliane had sat down abruptly. "That is splendid news," she said warmly. "Miss Lawley must have realized where her heart truly lay. And I am happy for Mr. Ardmore. Miss Lawley," she added wistfully, "has gained herself the kindest of men!"

After some moments of silence, she came back from a reverie to hear Lady Ailsa saying: "So you see, with Papa and Mamma soon to return, I must marry Gavin!"

"Oh, no," said Eliane, with what she hoped was an air of common sense and finality combined. "You cannot elope again! Remember what Lord Spendale threatened. The western tower at Glengarrick, I think he said?"

Surprisingly, Lady Ailsa did not respond. "You think I am jesting?" she said bitterly. "They *would* shut me up in Glengarrick Castle. And the western tower—ugh—you cannot know! There is nothing below the walls but the sea and rocks—such rocks!"

Miss Fielding kept her voice low. "Pray, Lady Ailsa, be sensible. His lordship would be very angry—"

"Don't you see that is the very point?" cried his sister. "I *will* marry Gavin, and I am terrified of Spendale's response. He has warned Gavin, and do you know what he can be like when he is really angry? He would not hesitate to kill Mr. Mackerras, and that is why I want your help. You are the only person who could halt him if he follows us—and I know he will. He finds out everything!"

"Oh, no, I cannot!" Eliane flushed and recoiled at the idea of being embroiled in Ailsa's mad quirks, of being sacrificed to the wrath of his lordship. "I could do nothing. I have no influence!" she protested.

"But you are so calm and sensible—you have the

greatest effect on him," pleaded Lady Ailsa. "He has the greatest respect for you. Why, only the other day he said he had never known anyone—" She stopped hastily as she recalled that her brother's precise words were that Miss Fielding was the most coldly resolute female it had been his lot to meet. She therefore paraphrased rapidly. "He said you had great coolness and resolution," she said.

"He—he said that?"

"Oh, do not say no, Eliane, I am desperate!"

"I am sorry, Lady Ailsa. I could not be party to this."

"Eliane, pray listen. You know that I love Gavin Mackerras to distraction. I will not be denied!" She got up from the bed and moved restlessly about the room, hugging her cloak around her, debating within herself. "You must help me to marry. I—I am going to have his child!"

"Dear Heaven, no." Eliane stared at her, utterly shocked. "Ailsa, how could you?"

"Now you see that I must marry him before he sails, and before my parents return, and why Spendale will almost certainly kill him unless you can deflect his wrath. Just be there—" she pleaded, "to delay him and give us time to escape if he should catch up with us!"

Eliane remained silent in distress and shock. She had not thought it of Mr. Mackerras, but the close parallel between Lady Ailsa's case and that of her own mother could not but have its effect upon her. *Her* mother had been wrenched from her husband to bear her child alone, confined in that great château on the banks of the Loire. And now poor little Ailsa was threatened with a similar fate in that bleak Scottish stronghold she had heard about.

Lady Ailsa could not have chosen a better conspirator. Eliane could have wrung her hands at the thought of meeting Spendale's fury, but she crossed the room to where Ailsa stood weeping, and put her arms about her and kissed her.

"There now, do not distress yourself! I will help you all I can. But what plans do we make?"

Lady Ailsa dabbed her tears dry and recovered resiliently.

"I have thought it out. I have warned you tonight so that you may be ready. You will tell no one, not even your father and mother? Bridie shall hire me a post chaise and four and I will come to collect you late tomorrow night. You can manage that?"

Eliane nodded dumbly. "And what of your brother?" she asked at last.

"I will give him the slip somehow, tomorrow night. I shall look very pale and say I have the headache if he wishes to take me out. But he goes gaming most nights, to places where he would never take me! Gaming—and worse, no doubt," she added resentfully. "The other night he came home beastly drunk, and oddly enough Spendale does not commonly drink to excess. It was the morning after that when he was fearfully out of sorts that he decided we should go up to Glengarrick!" She slid off the bed and replaced the pretty satin slippers whose jeweled heels flashed in the candlelight. "I must get back to Charlotte Mayo's. Spendale is there, but I left him playing faro, and that will keep his attention. I know for a fact that he has lost a prodigious amount lately. Now Eliane," as Miss Fielding reached for her dress, "pray do not trouble. I shall be quite all right. Perhaps your manservant will get me a chair—?"

Eliane stepped into her dress and wriggled hastily,

bidding her ladyship do up a few hooks. She thrust her feet into her shoes and put on a cloak and hood. "I am coming to see you on your way," she said firmly. "Molly shall accompany me, and she shall wake the boy to run beside your chair to Lady Mayo's. For you to have come here thus unattended was the height of folly."

This took but a few minutes, and they left the house as quietly as possible. Lady Ailsa leaned from her sedan chair.

"Until tomorrow," she whispered. "Good night to you, dearest Eliane!"

Dearest Eliane sighed deeply, and then hurried back with Molly. What had she let herself in for? On the other hand, what other course was open to her?

She spent a sleepless night, but the next day she packed a bag and hid it in a cupboard until she needed Molly to take it out to the chaise after midnight. She spent some painful moments writing a letter to her father, explaining that she had gone on a short journey with the Lady Ailsa Ardmore, and that she was sorry for the secret departure but had no choice. He was not to worry about her, and she would explain all when she returned in a few days.

She could not feel that this would do much to allay his fears at her extraordinary behavior, but she ended the letter by begging her dearest father to trust her. This missive she sealed heavily, and gave to Molly for later delivery. That evening Mr. and Mrs. Fielding were supping with friends, and Ned had arranged for some expedition of his own with Maria Taylor. Eliane excused herself from accompanying her parents and thankfully spent the evening alone. At last came the expected summons.

She saw with a feeling of exasperation that Lady Ailsa had seen fit to attire herself in a traveling dress of such high fashion that she would be rendered memorable to any innkeeper or servant along the route to Dover, and that she had managed to have smuggled out from Ardmore House a quantity of luggage which suggested that she might envisage traveling to India with the regiment.

The chaise moved away, and both girls fell silent. Through the city and over London Bridge they went and were making their way toward Kent when Lady Ailsa grew pale.

"I must confess," she said, "that now the die is cast, I feel a little sick."

"That will soon make two of us," said Miss Fielding from her corner of the swaying chaise. She pressed her gloved hand to her mouth. "As you may recall, I detest the motion of these vehicles."

Ailsa brightened. Her feeling of nausea was purely caused by apprehension and a feeling of guilt, and she momentarily forgot her sins in the remembrance of those of her brother.

"I remember!" she cried. "Spendale had to offer you brandy. Oh, what a comfort to think that *he* has sometimes taken a fall! He was so stricken that night to think he had misjudged what you were. I have never let him forget it!"

"I imagine," said Eliane severely and in some unexpected sympathy toward his lordship, "that he does not care to be reminded of it."

"Oh no," said his sister cheerfully. "It vexes him."

The chaise seemed to fly through the night. Lady Ailsa withdrew into her own thoughts, and Eliane, glancing at her pretty, willful face, wondered uneasily what would come next. She wished she had not revived memories of that evening at Hampstead. She had not long to wait.

"I have been thinking, Eliane, how I wish Spendale could have fallen in love with you—properly, I mean. You are such a dear, and he would make a famous husband."

Eliane closed her eyes. "Indeed?" she said with difficulty. "I thought you did not approve of him."

"Well, of course! But reformed rakes always make the best husbands, so they say. I shall not know, for"—delicacy caused her to blush a little—"for Mr. Mackerras is *not* a rake."

Eliane did not wish to pursue this point. She remained silent. Lady Ailsa, feeling the need to say something, chattered on. "If Spendale married for love, of course he would reform. If he does not, no doubt he will become as bad as ever, like that odious Sir Pelham Hodge, who is always pursuing me! He married the plainest woman, a duke's daughter, and has been the veriest pest to other females ever since. Now Spendale—"

"Lady Ailsa, if you wish me to continue this journey, you must cease talking of your brother!" cried the goaded Eliane.

"Oh, very well. I am sure I have no wish to think of him. Pray do not be cross, Eliane. No doubt you would much rather be thinking of Mr. Gretton. He seems a very agreeable young man."

Miss Fielding had no wish to discuss Mr. Gretton either. "Perhaps we should both endeavor to sleep a little," she suggested.

Through the night the horses' hooves pounded and the chaise jolted and swayed. Horses were changed at Westerham, at Tonbridge and again at Ashford, and at last they came to the end of their journey. It was now mid-afternoon.

Knowing that the town must be full, they stopped some way before Dover, at a village with a moderately sized coaching inn which could give them accommodation. The baggage was unloaded, and Lady Ailsa kept her word to send a message to Mr. Mackerras as to where she could be found. She now seemed in high spirits, although constantly listening for stopping traffic.

Miss Fielding ordered dinner, and found that she had little appetite compared with Lady Ailsa. As the serving maid cleared the table of their private parlor, her ladyship fixed Eliane with a thoughtful glance, and then said slowly:

"Eliane, my dearest, since we must soon expect Gavin to arrive, and I do not wish to enrage him, I must tell you that you must say nothing of—of the baby. It was not true."

Miss Fielding stared, as well she might.

"Of course, I have persuaded him to marry me, but the other—that was to make sure that you would come with me as far as Dover. I shall need you still to face Spendale, if that should be." She gave a nervous laugh. "No wonder you were surprised. As if Mr. Mackerras would ever be anything but the most honorable!"

"Lady Ailsa, I am more glad than I can say," breathed Eliane, "but my own feelings at the moment are strongly in favor of—of beating you! Your deception is beyond words! I remember you wept when you told me!"

"Oh, well, who would not? I cried because I felt guilty at telling such a fearful fib—but I have needed you, Eliane. That part is true. If Spendale traces us, you will see."

Eliane feared that indeed she would. She was inexpressibly relieved that Mr. Mackerras had not after all seduced Lady Ailsa, but gave vent to her feelings with some indignation "Ailsa, I begin to feel that the sooner you *are* married, the better!"

"Oh, that is splendid! Then we may be comfortable and await my darling Gavin!"

Lieutenant Mackerras duly arrived, in full regimentals. Somewhat embarrassed, he thanked Miss Fielding for her good offices. She wondered what pressures the willful Ailsa had brought to bear upon him to cause him to agree to this hasty marriage, but concluded that she must have misjudged his caution. He was undoubtedly in love, and faced with a long parting, and possibly a final one. He had in fact been busy at his end, and had been to the Bishop to procure a special license. If he should fall foul of his Colonel and lose his hardly bought commission, he was prepared for that. He could see little hope of advancement in the Army, and was already thinking of the East India Company. If he were to be married to Lady Ailsa Ardmore, he would need all the drive and ambition of an impoverished Scot.

That night, at the rectory, the ceremony was performed, and for better or worse, richer or poorer, in sickness and in health, Lady Ailsa became the wife of Gavin Mackerras. They looked so utterly happy that Eliane retired to her room, feeling that she could not have wished them any other outcome.

The busy inn stirred to life early next morning, but throughout the clatter and clamor of voices and horses and heavy wheels, the newlyweds and the hitherto sleepless Miss Fielding slept on. She breakfasted alone, in mid-morning, but they came down to dinner and joined her.

"Gavin must return tomorrow," said Lady Ailsa. "The regiment is embarking, and the wind is in the right quarter."

They had so much to talk about still, their future so very much in question, that Eliane sympathized with their desire to be alone. She said that she would stay in the inn while they took a walk. She watched them leave the inn, making as pretty a picture as would melt a heart of stone.

She sat alone in the downstairs parlor, a book in her hand, but unable to concentrate. How long, she thought, before her ladyship's absence was discovered? What, even now, was Lord Spendale doing? If only Lieutenant Mackerras could gain permission to take Lady Ailsa aboard with him, as she had obviously intended he should do! Then Miss Fielding with her guilty secret might journey back to London, and hope that her complicity might never be discovered!

There was so much traffic to and from Dover that she had almost forgotten to listen to every new arrival. Suddenly there was a sickening lurch within her as she heard his voice, and the answering murmur of the innkeeper.

The book fell from her lap. There was a firm step outside in the stone-flagged passage, and then Spendale came into the parlor with his long stride.

He had obviously ridden post, and his riding boots and buckskins were spattered with mud. He was gripping his riding whip, but her frightened eyes saw that beneath his coat he wore a sword.

He halted sharply, expecting to see his sister, and

instead seeing the one person in the world he had not expected.

"My God!" he said. "You!"

She could not answer. The sudden quick look of pleasure in his face had been replaced equally suddenly by anger, as he realized what must be the reason for her surprising presence. Her spirit quailed. She knew with instant hopelessness that it had been useless to think she might stay his fury, and she herself had now become one of the enemy. He could only regard her presence as treachery. Indeed, his next words confirmed it.

"I had not expected this!" he said contemptuously. "Where is my sister?"

"She—she is—not here, Lord Spendale."

"She has left—with Mackerras? No—there would be no point. He must remain in Dover until the regiment sails." He paced angrily. "I would have been here before now but for some infernal fool at the War Department who misdirected me as to where his regiment lay! But I have seen his Colonel, and I know they are here!" He flung her an outraged glance. "I did not expect to see you! You have done this to spite me! But I did not think it of Mackerras, either! I trusted him, and he has made a fool of me. Well, I warned him before of the consequences, and now he will answer for it. Where is he, Madam?"

"Not—not here," she stammered. "Nor your sister."

"I should expect you to lie, but I will soon see!" he snapped. "Away from that doorway, if you please!"

She was suddenly fearful that the newlyweds might have returned by the back stairway, and she stayed where she was. "Lord Spendale, pray calm yourself. It is too late. Mr. Mackerras and your sister are married."

"Married! Already? Well, she shall be unmarried soon enough! I warned him." His hand had gone instinctively to the hilt of his sword.

"Lord Spendale, they are *married*," she stressed the word bravely. "They married yesterday. It is too late. It cannot be undone."

She was terrified of his fury.

"Damnation! How am I to face my father? I gave him my word that she should come to no harm, and Mackerras has made a liar out of me! He shall pay for that, by God! *Are you going to get out of my way?*"

She stood back against the door, blocking his passage. He did not attempt to remove her as she feared, but the next moment she had removed herself as she received a stinging buffet which made her head sing. He ran swiftly up the inn stairs to search the upper rooms, and as swiftly came down again, never glancing at her and went out into the inn yard. She heard his horse move away, and put up a trembling hand to her reddening face.

Then she remembered that Gavin and Ailsa had only gone for a stroll, and could not be far away. Heedless of the press of people in the outer taproom, and the mark of the blow on her face, she hurried through out into the inn yard. She asked an ostler if he knew which way the lady and gentleman staying in the inn had gone.

He pointed the way with a grin, having just answered the same question a moment before.

Eliane gathered up her skirts and began to run along the roadway. A quarter of a mile uphill, stumbling, running, walking, brought her to where the road ran along the side of the hill, and to the chilling sound of a scream which must have come from Lady Ailsa. She hurried on, now hearing the sound of clashing sword blades. She saw Spendale's tethered horse, its head drooping tiredly, and just below the road, a small flat dip where Ailsa and her husband had gone to stand and take a long look at the Kent countryside below them.

Now she came to where the two men fought, a few feet below the level of the road. Lady Ailsa stood back, well out of the way, wringing her hands and choking back her cries. Lord Spendale's sister had no doubt about the outcome, but saw no way to halt them. Men had their own code in such matters and she feared to interrupt that swift swordplay. Gavin would not thank her, and she could only bite her hands and sob.

Miss Fielding looked on in horror. She had never before seen men fighting, and the steel blades looked the murderous instruments they were. Lunge—parry—riposte—the flash and clash of blades and the near silent scrape of their feet on the sandy soil, the hard breathing of both men.... Their desperate obscene purpose was a nightmare to Eliane. She could see that Mr. Mackerras was having to give way. He was being forced to give ground as they circled, fighting viciously. As Mackerras backed, they came closer to where Miss Fielding stood agonizedly above them on the roadway.

"Stop—oh, stop," she cried, with little confidence that they would even hear her, let alone respond. In her anxiety, she leaned forward, and the hawthorn bush upon whose half exposed roots she stood, gave a little, and the sandy subsoil began to avalanche down toward the antagonists.

Miss Fielding went with it, hurtling those few feet toward the flashing blades.

"Eliane!" shouted Spendale and instinctively put up his blade. Gavin Mackerras, tired and beaten as he was, had not such swift reactions as his opponent. He had already completed his lunge before he could draw back, and his sword went through the unguarded body of his lordship.

This time Lady Ailsa's shrieks reached hysteria. Eliane, jarred and shaken by her fall, looked up to see Spendale crumple, the blood already staining near his heart. And Gavin Mackerras, his reddened blade in his hand, stared aghast at his wife.

Mr. Mackerras, the soldier, remained frozen only for a moment. The next instant he was kneeling beside the injured man, wrenching off his own cravat and rolling it into a pad to thrust against the wound. With trembling hands the girls ripped their petticoats for bandages, both silent now, and white of face.

"Not your fault...." said Spendale faintly and his eyes closed. Satisfied with his first aid, Gavin Mackerras ran toward Spendale's horse, Ailsa following distractedly. "I'll ride back to the inn for a conveyance, and send to the surgeon, Ailsa. Do you stay with him."

Eliane knelt beside him, holding his hand. "Oh, my love, forgive me—I have killed you," she breathed.

He was drifting into unconsciousness, and did not appear to be aware of her. Then he opened his eyes as he struggled back sufficiently to say what he must. "Eliane—no blame to Mackerras," he said faintly. "You will testify?"

"Yes, oh, yes," she sobbed.

Mr. Mackerras reached the inn, and there enlisted the help of a young gentleman who had halted a smart chaise and pair. Together they returned and lifted in the now unconscious man. The two girls insisted on walking back so that there might be more room for Lord Spendale, and by the time they reached the inn, his lordship had been put to bed and the surgeon sent for.

There now began an hour by hour battle for his life. Gavin the soldier was best equipped to deal with something of which the ladies had no experience, although either of them would willingly have died to undo the harm which had been done. They hovered, silent and frightened, outside the door of his room until Gavin came out with the surgeon.

"How is he?" sobbed Ailsa. "Is he dead?"

"Why, no, your ladyship, nor likely to be, if all goes well," said the doctor reassuringly. "The blade has gone through his lordship's ribs, but appears to have missed his heart and lungs. We may save him yet."

He had lost a great deal of blood, and a fever rapidly set in. The young gentleman with the chaise, who was on his way to London, undertook to call at Ardmore House and arrange for Leckie to come. Until further help came, Eliane took her turn at watching him through the night, bathing his forehead and frightened at his increasing restlessness, fearing that all their efforts would fail to halt the hemorrhage. She sat beside his bed, desperately watching his beloved face, willing him not to die....

CHAPTER ELEVEN

THE next day they hoped to have succeeded in stopping the hemorrhage, but the fever continued to mount. They took turns in nursing him, each of them oppressed by feelings of guilt for the mishap. Lady Ailsa felt it to be the direct result of her selfish desire to marry her lover at all costs. Mr. Mackerras similarly reproached himself for so nearly depriving his darling wife of her favorite brother, and Miss Fielding felt a double responsibility. She felt she should never have assisted the naughty Ailsa in the first place, and worst of all was her unlucky attempt to halt the duel which had only brought about a disaster for which she was so humiliatingly to blame.

The curious thing was that none of the three attached any blame at all to the victim. Mr. Mackerras, whom he had plainly sought to send into the next world, only considered that his lordship had done what any other man of honor would do. He had no option, in his code, but to act thus from his failure to honor his promise to his father that he would protect his sister.

On the third day, it seemed as if his great natural vitality was enabling Lord Spendale to hold his own. Unless something untoward occurred, he must begin to mend, Gavin assured the girls.

Leckie had arrived and took his turn at nursing his master. Eliane went down to the parlor to make an effort to eat her supper while Gavin rode into Dover on a hasty visit to his brother officers. Having procured writing materials from the landlord, Eliane left her meal largely untouched and sat down to write to her father. At last Lady Ailsa came down to speak to her, and found the letter half written and Eliane in tears, which she tried instantly to hide.

"Oh, Eliane, please do not weep! It is not your fault. You have nothing to reproach yourself with!"

Miss Fielding dabbed her eyes and tried to speak steadily. "How does he progress?"

"He is still a little delirious, I think. He keeps muttering and turning restlessly, which makes one a little afraid the wound will reopen. Gavin says he and Leckie will sit by him tonight, that you and I may get some sleep. I suppose he is right. Eliane!"

For Miss Fielding had turned away with shaking shoulders. Ailsa regarded her distress for a moment, while a light broke upon her. "Eliane, how blind I have been. You love my brother—of course you do! Oh, how stupid I have been not to see! I had been so sure it was Mr. Gretton! Have you always—?"

"Always," said Eliane, and felt an enormous relief at being able to say it at last, to his sister if not to himself. "N-nearly always," she added, incurably honest.

Lady Ailsa gazed at her, telling herself once again

how foolish she had been not to guess. She wondered what else she had failed to see. "Does he love you also, Eliane?"

"No," said Miss Fielding loyally, but her full heart impelled her to add: "N-not any m-more."

Her ladyship took this to mean that her brother's first attraction to someone he had sought to make his mistress had not been renewed in a more acceptable fashion. She felt she was on very delicate ground, and sought to change the subject a little.

She mentioned that they would be needing fresh lint soon, and Eliane immediately offered to go next day into Dover to find an apothecary's shop where any necessities might be got.

The next morning, the rector and his wife very kindly offered to take her in their coach as they had calls to make in the town. Mr. Mackerras having obtained an extension of his leave from his duties, remained with his wife. Seeing how pale and tired she looked he persuaded her to go out of the inn for some air, and Lady Ailsa with unaccustomed meekness did as she was bid, but did not go in the direction of Dover, near the dell where the hideous combat had taken place. It would always be a memory of horror for Ailsa.

She walked in the opposite direction, glad to miss the constant traffic in the inn yard. She returned to see that the place was no quieter, for a London bound coach-and-six had halted, piled high with luggage, its passengers standing by in the inn yard. She gave it half a glance, and continued her way to the inn door.

The Channel crossing had proved disagreeable to Lady Glengarrick. The Earl and Countess had returned from France in company with a French gentleman whose hospitality they were to return in London, and would have preferred to spend a day in Dover itself before beginning the journey back to town, but Dover being full they had failed to find accommodation. By the time they had got to Buckland, the Earl of Glengarrick, glancing at his wife, had ordered the coachman to stop at the next likely looking inn.

Lady Ailsa noticed the French fashions of some of the party, but registered little else until her face went red with shock as she was confronted by the being she most feared and respected in all the world.

"Papa!"

Lord Glengarrick surveyed his younger daughter, noted her distraught air, and said in measured tones: "Ailsa?"

"Oh, Papa! Thank Heaven you are here." Frightened though she was, he was her father and the source of all strength and security, and careless of onlookers she flung herself at him and wound her arms around his neck. "Oh, Papa, we are in terrible trouble. Spendale has nearly died and it is all my fault!"

Glengarrick's glance had become very sharp indeed as he detached her from his person. However, he merely said: "Perhaps we had better inquire into this inside? But first, your duty to your mother."

Lady Ailsa looked hastily for her mother, and saw her standing with the French gentleman, her eyes upon her daughter in urgent questioning.

"Mamma—" She sank down in the graceful curtsy to which she had been trained, and then went toward her parent, expecting her usual kiss. Lady Glengarrick remained grave. "What is this, Ailsa? Is Spendale here?"

"Yes, Mamma. Oh, Mamma—"

Lady Glengarrick took her daughter's left hand, and raised her eyes from the bright gold band that graced it. "Take your father and me to your room, Ailsa," she said coldly.

She turned and spoke rapidly to the elderly Frenchman, who bowed and followed her into the inn. Upstairs, Gavin Mackerras continued his vigil in Spendale's room, while in their room, Lady Ailsa faced her parents alone.

"And now, Ailsa?" said her father.

Her face puckered, but she gathered her courage. "I have disobeyed you, Papa, and married Mr. Mackerras. Spendale followed us here, and he and Gavin fought," she gave a convulsive sob. "Oh, Papa, Mamma, forgive me—forgive me—"

It seemed to Katrine Glengarrick that she had heard those words many times before. It was her youngest child pleading that she should not be faced with the consequences of her willfulness. But this time, Ailsa could not evade responsibility. Since neither parent spoke, the girl sank down into a chair, and sobbed with genuine heartbreak.

Lord Glengarrick turned to his wife. "I see, my dear, that we stayed too long. I confess I had thought to see Spendale manage better than this!"

Ailsa raised a tearstained but indignant face. "It is *not* his fault, Papa," she said loyally. "He has been wholly admirable—in looking after me. It is I who am at fault. I deceived him, and if you cannot forgive me, you are not to be angry with Alastair. As for the duel, I think he would have killed Gavin—I don't know—but the accident happened when Miss Fielding," she broke off, not sure how she should involve Eliane, and anxious that nothing should be said that would reflect to her brother's discredit. "She fell from the road above, and Spendale put up his sword and Gavin ran him through—it happened in a second—it was not her fault—nor Gavin's either," she started to sob again.

"You would all appear to be singularly blameless," remarked Lord Glengarrick, "and if Spendale has indeed been wholly admirable, then he must have changed in my absence!"

Lady Glengarrick said in her gentle voice: "You must tell us more clearly, Ailsa. Who is it that fell?"

"M-Miss Fielding. She was with me—I persuaded her—oh, I have been wicked, wicked!"

"No doubt we shall understand eventually," said her father. "In the meantime, where and how is Spendale? Who is with him now?"

"Gavin, Papa. We have all tried to save him, and please, oh please do not be too angry with Gavin. We do love each other truly, and he will make me a very good husband, I swear it."

"You are not required to swear anything," said her father. "I suppose these are the habits of speech you have been acquiring in London. As for your husband, I shall have something to say to him later. Katrine, will you wait while I see Spendale?"

"Yes." She looked up at him. "But do not keep me long, Glengarrick."

Their eyes met in secret understanding. Lady Margaret's guess had been shrewd. Katrine Glengarrick had a special protective regard for her difficult eldest son.

"Come, Ailsa, direct me to your brother."

In the quiet room at the back of the inn, Mr. Mackerras received the jolt of his life as his wife's father walked in, but beyond a frigid acknowledgment of his startled "Sir!" Glengarrick ignored him and went to look at the flushed face of his heir. Spendale slept, but restlessly. Glengarrick's face was impassive.

"What is his injury?"

He listened to Gavin's explanation. "Do not disturb him," he said. "I will bring his mother."

He went out, and Ailsa flew into her husband's arms for comfort. "He is angry, Gavin, and he will never endure to have Mamma upset, but as *he* loves *her*, so he must come to understand how we feel!" She looked toward the bed where her brother lay. "Oh, how I wish it had never happened! Perhaps he never meant to kill you, Gavin, but only make it an affair of honor—you did not mean to kill him, either!"

To Lieutenant Mackerras it seemed that he had been fighting for his life, but he said nothing to disillusion her.

Lord Glengarrick had gone to take his wife to see their son. "He is ill, Katrine, but not, I think, dying. Ailsa has as usual exaggerated, so take heart!"

Lady Glengarrick went to her son's room and gazed at him, resting her hand on her husband's arm. "What a mercy that I felt unwell and we stopped here," she said. She became aware of Mr. Mackerras, who bowed low.

"Lady Glengarrick, your ladyship's most obedient and humble servant," he said.

"Mr. Mackerras," she inclined her head politely. "How is my son?"

"I think he does well, Ma'am. It is the fourth day, and we have halted the hemorrhage, I think. Believe me, Ma'am, I can never sufficiently express my regret that the accident should have happened."

She looked at him. "You have done very wrong, Mr. Mackerras."

Gavin Mackerras accepted the reproof, but stood his ground. "Lady Glengarrick," he said in a low voice, "with regard to Lord Spendale, I am truly devastated that this unlucky mishap should have occurred. But for that unfortunate occurrence, he would certainly have dispatched me! I was no match for him." He included the Earl of Glengarrick now in his glance. "As for my marriage to your daughter, I do indeed regret the circumstances, but not the fact. I can only hope that you will forgive us as I make her happy."

Lord Glengarrick returned him no reply, except to say that they must not disturb Spendale, and they withdrew.

After Lady Glengarrick had retired to rest, and her husband had assured himself that his party were accommodated with reasonable comfort, he sent a summons to Mr. Mackerras.

It seemed to the waiting Ailsa that it was a long interview. Unable to bear the suspense alone, she went to her own room, where her mother was resting, and tapped on the door. "Mamma? It is Ailsa. May I come in?"

Lady Glengarrick bade her enter. She looked less pale than formerly, and patted a chair beside the bed. "Now, Ailsa, sit here and tell me what has been happening. From the beginning, please."

Lady Ailsa obliged, but was careful not to mention her previous escapade. She accounted for her acquaintance with Miss Fielding by telling her mother the same story they had invented for Eliane's father.

"I cannot approve very much of this young woman, Ailsa. She does not appear to me to have enough principle. She should never have encouraged your disobedience by accompanying you."

"But, Mamma, I—I misled her a little. Please do not ask me how. I am ashamed. She acted out of kindness to me. Mamma, she is the most admirable person, and I love her dearly. And she is *devoted* to Spendale!"

"Indeed?" Lady Glengarrick's fine brows rose questioningly.

"Yes, Mamma. She has nursed him devotedly. She tried to stop the duel. That is how the accident happened. In fact, she loves him to distraction!"

"Indeed," said her mother again. "And does Spendale return this regard?"

"No—at least—er—no, Mamma, he does not. And I am sorry for it, because she would make him a most admirable wife, except she has no family nor fortune. But her father is a gentleman, I am sure. Mamma, it might be that Spendale considers the distance between them too great, since he is heir to Glengarrick, but it is a pity—"

Katrine Glengarrick looked thoughtfully at her daughter's earnest face. Willful and self-centered Ailsa might be, but she was no fool either. This new acquaintance had an ardent advocate. "I shall be interested to see your Miss Fielding," she said calmly. "And now perhaps you will tell me of Mr. Mackerras, and how you prevailed upon an honorable young man to behave dishonorably."

"Oh, Mamma!" said Ailsa, and burst into tears.

Nevertheless, she checked her sobs and began to speak. If Lady Glengarrick was not, within the next ten minutes, wholly reconciled to the alliance with Mr. Mackerras, it was not the fault of her daughter. Feeling somewhat battered by her fervor, she said at last that that was enough for now, and they had better take another look at Spendale.

Miss Fielding's return from Dover was considerably delayed by the length of the rector's calls. She went straight to her room with her purchases and was surprised to find Lady Ailsa there waiting for her. She set the parcel of lint and ointments and lavender water upon the table and said a little anxiously: "I hope the inn will not prove too noisy tonight. There is a coach-and-six unloading in the yard."

"Eliane! You cannot guess! It is Mamma and Papa returned from France! Mamma was a little unwell with the crossing and they stopped here. Is it not providential?" Rapidly she explained. "So now Mamma will stay here to look after Spendale—oh, dear, I wonder how Gavin is managing with Papa, who can be most terrifying when he is angry!"

Miss Fielding thought involuntarily of someone else who had that ability also. She said quickly, to banish a memory, "No doubt your husband will make his peace, Ailsa."

She untied the parcel with deliberate care. "Well, now that Lady Glengarrick is here, there will be no need for me to remain with you. I will arrange to return to London as soon as possible."

"Oh, must you, Eliane? I suppose you feel you must. I have been selfish long enough. But I have told Mamma you are here, so you will dine with us all tonight? Dinner is bespoken for seven in the big parlor. There is a French gentleman who came with Papa, so do not fear that too much will be said of family matters," she added reassuringly.

That evening Eliane was thankful that she had

obeyed the impulse to pack the ivory watered silk when she had left Soho. The sapphires she had worn at Ardmore House were naturally still in her father's keeping, but they would not have been suitable for display at an inn. Hastily she called the chambermaid to help her dress and to do her hair. Nothing loth, the country girl helped to pile the dark curls high, and both of them were well pleased with their efforts as she prepared to descend to join the company in the big parlor.

She did not know what to expect, but as she entered she found only Lady Ailsa and her father, Mr. Mackerras and the elderly Frenchman.

She found, as she sank gracefully before the Earl of Glengarrick, that he was not an older version of Spendale. It was Neil Ardmore who resembled his father. Deep blue eyes surveyed her shrewdly, but with courtesy.

"Your humble servant, Miss Fielding. I am deeply sensible of your good offices toward my errant family. I hope I may express my thanks at greater length, but first may I present M. le Marquis de Varency, who is to be my guest in London."

M. le Marquis had risen to his feet at her entry. He had been watching her with great interest, and now it seemed that as he bowed, a little stiff with age, but with great elegance and courtesy, Miss Fielding herself had forgotten her manners. She stood rooted to the spot, not with deliberate discourtesy, but because her limbs would not obey her commands. Her face had drained of color, but she strove for composure.

"M'sieu," and now gave him the deepest court curtsy, worthy of Versailles itself, but her face, it seemed to the astonished Lady Ailsa, had assumed an icy hauteur that did not seem to belong to the Eliane she knew.

M. le Marquis de Varency came forward toward his granddaughter. "Eliane? You are *la petite* Eliane? I cannot be mistaken. The name, and you have your mother's features!"

He had spoken in French, and she replied, in the faultless accent Mr. Fielding had taken so much care to preserve. There was still an icy dignity in her manner which did her no disservice in her grandfather's eyes.

He turned to his host. "You present to me Miss Fielding, Lord Glengarrick. May I present to you my granddaughter, whom I find so unexpectedly soon?"

It seemed to Eliane that a babble of talk arose about her ears. She found herself being kissed by Lady Ailsa, who then loudly wondered what could be detaining Mamma, who must be told of this wonder immediately. Eliane was then taken aside by Lord Glengarrick, who said with great kindliness that she must wish to be seated next her grandfather, and that they must be left to develop their acquaintance. He asked his daughter to restrain her delight and not to overwhelm her mother the moment she entered.

Lady Glengarrick came in, and Eliane saw that it was she from whom Lady Ailsa and Spendale got their dark good looks. Miss Fielding was presented as Miss Fielding, with no immediate mention of the sensation which had just been caused. The Marquis asked politely after the invalid.

Katrine Glengarrick smiled her relief and pleasure. "He does well, I thank you, M'sieu. He knew me, for at least some of the time." She allowed herself to be seated, and looking at the company around the table, explained a little more. "He is still a little feverish, I think. He wanders a little. He seems to be very worried because he has *hit* someone!"

"Indeed, Mamma," cried Ailsa, "he has a heavy hand. He has boxed my ears more than once."

"It seems strange that that should bother him," said her father. He turned to his son-in-law. "That duty now falls upon you, Mr. Mackerras."

Eliane hoped that her burning cheeks would escape notice in the general exchange of good-humored pleasantries. It was plain that the Earl of Glengarrick had come to an understanding with his son-in-law and that Lady Ailsa was no longer in the deepest disgrace. They spoke of Lord Spendale's condition for a while, and the necessity of removing him to London as soon as possible, and then Lady Ailsa could contain herself no longer.

"Mamma—it is the happiest circumstance! It is Miss Fielding who is—who is—"

"My granddaughter, Madame," said the Marquis with a bow.

The chatter of amazement began all over again, but it seemed that Lady Glengarrick knew something of the history of the former Mlle. de Varency, and skillfully and with great delicacy kept the conversation in unembarrassing channels.

However much she tried that evening, Eliane could not feel at ease with her French grandfather, no matter how courtly his manner. To her he was and must surely always be the terrible old man who had separated her parents before she was born in order to avenge his ferocious family pride. Nevertheless, she could not but be sensible of the mellowing effect of age upon him. He had responded to her father's overtures of peace in a manner she found astounding. He had made an effort to come to seek her himself, not summoning her father imperiously to France. She who had always been secretly aware of her true inheritance, was now concerned to stress very much that she was English, the daughter of Charles Fielding, English by nationality and upbringing, even though her clear and rapid French undoubtedly pleased M. le Marquis de Varency.

When future plans were discussed, and the Marquis made it understandably plain that he did not wish to remain at an English wayside inn, but preferred to travel on to London, Eliane quietly resisted all suggestions that she should travel with him. She made every excuse she could, chiefly that her father would have received her letter before her return, and might well have started for Dover himself. In her resistance, she was grateful for the support of Lady Glengarrick, who said with her calm air that M. le Marquis must have much to attend to in London, that there was no hurry at all, and she would be glad to have Miss Fielding's company for a day or so, as would her daughter. They would, she said, all return to Park Lane as soon as her son's condition permitted his removal.

So the next day, M. de Varency departed for London in the coach-and-six, taking with him his own and some of Lord Glengarrick's servants and much of the baggage of the tour. The coach was then to return to Dover.

After she had respectfully seen her grandfather on his journey, the inn seemed to Eliane a less oppressive place. Ailsa and her husband were to join his regiment at least until he had resigned his commission to join the East India Company, having decided, with the concurrence of his father-in-law, to enter trade. Lady Ailsa was in high spirits, and could not wait to tell her brother the news. Eliane hastily made the request that she would not tell him of her own family history, and the surprised Lady Ailsa gave her reluctant word that she would not. Miss Fielding herself would have been hard put to it to say exactly why she did not wish this revelation to be made to Lord Spendale, but it had something to do with an instinctive desire that he should not now feel impelled to offer once more for her as amends for his latest reprehensible behavior.

Eliane did not feel she could impose any such request upon his parents. It seemed an impertinence to appear to assume that they might be interested enough in her affairs to comment upon them to their son. They must surely have much more to say to him on their own concerns after their long absence. They must wish to speak of their tour, of Lady Margaret and her baby son, and of Neil Ardmore and his betrothal to Miss Lawley.

In response to an inquiry from Lady Ailsa as to what she intended to do that morning, Eliane made the excuse that she was engaged to visit the rectory, after she had bidden farewell to Lady Ailsa herself and Mr. Mackerras. Ailsa nodded thoughtfully, and went into her brother's room to bid him farewell also.

Lord Spendale was undoubtedly recovering fast. Still pale and weak, his fever had gone, and his eyes held their old teasing as he viewed his sister's extravagant traveling dress, and bade her behave herself in her new role.

Ailsa pulled idly at the curling plumes of her enchanting hat, and then sat beside him, saying in her best wheedling tone: "Spendale, you may rest assured that I shall never reveal to anyone how we came to be acquainted with Miss Fielding—"

His eyes sharpened. "You will oblige me by forgetting it entirely, Ailsa. I have come to hold Miss Fielding in the highest regard. You know she is beyond reproach." He saw that his sister's gaze was one of expectancy. "If you must know, I have besought her many times to marry me, but she will not."

Lady Ailsa nearly jumped with surprise. "You—you have? Oh, if she is not the slyest creature—no, no, pray don't look like that! Of course she is the dearest girl! But she said nothing of this to me! Only that she loves *you*!"

"Ailsa! When did she say that?"

"Why—I found her weeping when you were ill—she said she had always loved you, though to be sure, I don't think you have deserved it!"

"Neither have I!" But he looked happier than she had seen him for some time.

"Alastair—there is one matter I must clear up before I go with Gavin. This affair of Eliane being here with me. You know, she would not have accompanied me—she utterly refused, until I deceived her."

"Oh?"

"Y-yes." Ailsa had the grace to go scarlet. "I told her I had to marry Gavin because I was pregnant. It wasn't true—not at all—but it made her come to support me. I wanted her to help me face you if you followed us, as you did. I knew you would be in a rage, because of Papa."

"Oh, my poor darling," he said softly. To his sister he said: "Ailsa, words fail me. You truly beggar description! What sort of wife are you going to make your unfortunate husband?"

"Oh, as to that," said Lady Ailsa cheerfully, "I have decided it all. I shall be loving, and sensible, and—and *obedient*!"

Passing quietly by his room on her way out of the inn, Eliane heard his deep laugh, which broke off abruptly as his mirth tore at his wound. How glad she was to hear him—he must be greatly relieved that his sister's problems had resolved themselves and that his parents had safely returned. Feeling nevertheless oddly depressed and lonely, in spite of a newly acquired grandfather of such eminence, she determined not to hurry back from the rectory. In fact, if she could induce the rector's wife to offer her dinner, she would not return until later that afternoon or evening. Lord and Lady Glengarrick must wish to be alone with their son, and she did not wish to be in the way. Perhaps tomorrow her father would arrive.

The Earl and Countess were not displeased to find themselves alone after their daughter's excited departure. They partook of the best midday dinner that the inn could provide, leaving Spendale to further healing slumbers.

"What are we to do about him, Philip? Miss Fielding has plainly taken herself off out of the way. In spite of what Ailsa has told us, they have plainly quarreled. She seems to be a most estimable young woman in every way. Is there anything we can do?"

"Nothing," said the Earl of Glengarrick. He smiled at her still lovely face, now wearing its habitual expression of concern when her eldest son and his activities were discussed. "He must come to know his own mind, and mend his ways. If anything needs to be said, you may safely leave it to me."

Katrine was content, but as the afternoon hours

passed, she began to look a little anxiously for Miss Fielding's return. Eliane came back from the rectory with some books for Spendale to while away his convalescent hours, and Lady Glengarrick expressed her pleasure, adding in her calm way: "My son was in fact asking if he might see you, Miss Fielding. He will be grateful for the books, I am sure."

Eliane went to her room to wash and change her dress. It had to be the ivory silk again, because she had no other, but she knew it became her very well. It had memories too of that supper party at Ardmore House where she had first seen a Spendale more to her taste, where she had in fact begun to know herself in love with him.

At last, with some agitation, since she had not seen him since his fever had left him, she tapped on the door of his room and in response to his call entered. Her dark blue eyes met his across the room. He was obviously much better, still pale with the loss of so much blood, but he looked very much himself as he leaned back against the pillows. His left arm was still bandaged to his side, but he looked immaculate and comfortable in a fine lawn shirt with the most elegant of ruffles.

She began to wonder how he would greet her, for as yet he had done nothing but gaze at her as she stood there, a little uncertain of him. Hurriedly, she said. "Good evening, Lord Spendale. I—I have brought you some books from the rector."

Spendale said at last: "I hit you."

She moved then, like one released from enchantment, and came to set the books on the little table beside him.

She nodded. "Hard."

He held out one hand toward her. "You see, I can *never* make you love me!"

She said, half in tears and half smiling: "You cannot know how greatly you have succeeded!"

There was a glimmer of a smile in the hazel eyes. "That was nobly said. Eliane, I have indeed been stupid and arrogant, as you once charged me. I have a vile temper. I shall never deserve you, and yet how I need you, my lovely, delicate Eliane! Will you take me as I am?" His free hand, so much thinner and yet still strong, held hers. "Darling, I was never more serious in my life. Say that you love me and will marry me, to give me courage to defy my father. You would never believe that he has chosen this—this of all times, to tell me he has found a wife for me—" He moved restlessly. "Once I might have obliged him but not now! It is too much! I have told him I must choose for myself! But he will take it hard, coming after Ailsa's tricks."

Was this, then, why she had been feeling so desolate all day? "This—this wife he has fixed upon," she stammered, with sinking heart.

"Some infernal Frenchman my parents brought over from France! He has a granddaughter I am to offer for! They were at this inn—you must have seen them, but no matter, I will not! I do not care how 'delightful' she may be, how suitable in every way!" He broke off, regarding her radiant face with puzzlement. "Eliane?"

"Oh, Alastair, did your father say that? I shall love him as I love my own! Don't you see? If your father said that, it was his way of giving us his blessing—and teasing you a little—"

He stared a moment longer, and then smiled. "So!" he said. "Your French mother—she was Mlle. de

Varency! And that explains so much. The sapphires that puzzled me—they were hers?"

"Yes."

"But you knew all the time—of your parentage?"

"Yes—except—well, never mind. My father seldom spoke of her—he cared so much. I—I cannot as yet like my grandfather, but he has at least sought my father—"

Was either of them really listening to what she was saying? Spendale leaned back against the pillows.

"Kiss me," he commanded.

She obeyed, and kissed him gently upon the lips. He received it passively, like an absolution and a benediction, returning only the faintest pressure. "I needed that," he said soberly, and then, with his one good arm encircling her waist, he proceeded, for an invalid, to manage very well on his own account.

ABOUT THE AUTHOR

KATHARINE FLIXTON lives in London.

*R*egency presents the popular and prolific...
JOAN SMITH

Available at your bookstore or use this coupon.

___AURORA	21533	$2.95
___DRURY LANE DARLING	21500	$2.95
___HERMIT'S DAUGHTER	21588	$2.95
___IMPRUDENT LADY	23663	$2.95
___LARCENOUS LADY	21261	$2.50
___LOVE'S HARBINGER	20955	$2.50
___MEMOIRS OF A HOYDEN	21329	$2.50
___ROYAL SCAMP	21610	$2.95
___SILKEN SECRETS	21372	$2.95

FAWCETT MAIL SALES
Dept. TAF, 201 E. 50th St., New York, N.Y. 10022

Please send me the FAWCETT BOOKS I have checked above. I am enclosing $............(add $2.00 to cover postage and handling for the first book and 50¢ each additional book). Send check or money order—no cash or C.O.D.'s please. Prices are subject to change without notice. Valid in U.S. only. All orders are subject to availability of books.

Name_____

Address_____

City_____ State_____ Zip Code_____

Allow at least 4 weeks for delivery.   TAF-67